"Who are you?"

A tiny jab of her kni... man who'd snuck int... ...punctuated Jane's question.

"Dr. Harker?"

She frowned. American accent–upper Midwest from the sound of him. Definitely military, but what was he doing in Quintana Roo, Mexico?

"You are Dr. Harker?" he pressed.

Jane nodded. If he was going to kill her, he was going to kill her, regardless of who she was. She'd seen his face. A very nice face beneath several days' growth of dark beard–handsome if you went for Clint Eastwood before too many years in the sun and wind had taken their toll. She didn't–but that didn't mean she couldn't appreciate good-looking when she saw it.

"Grab what you need," he snapped. "We have to get out of here before the guards return." He glanced out the door. "I'd rather not kill them if I don't have to."

"Listen, soldier boy, there'll be no killing. There's been enough."

"Works for me. Now, let's go."

Dear Reader,

Welcome back to the continuing saga of THE LUCHETTI BROTHERS. This time it's Bobby's turn.

What happens when Bobby Luchetti returns home to discover one of his brothers has broken their cardinal rule—never touch your brother's girl?

Since Bobby is a member of the elite Special Forces unit Delta Force, he accepts a mission to rescue Dr. Jane Harker, a kidnapped senator's daughter. What follows is a story I like to think of as *Romancing the Stone* meets *The American President*.

How do two brothers find their way back to being brothers? And how does Bobby find both the life he was meant to lead and the woman he was meant to share it with? The usual way—trial and a whole lot of error.

Bobby and Jane save each other in more ways than one. They discover that love is found in the strangest of places and forever is worth all the trouble it takes to get there. With repeat visits from most of the Luchettis, as well as their pets, and a brand-new Mexican stray named Lucky, *A Soldier's Quest* should have something for everyone.

Next up, Tim Luchetti decides it's time for him to find a mommy and for Dean to find love. Find out who wins both their hearts in *The Mommy Quest*.

I'd also like to invite you to check out another series I'm writing. If you enjoyed *Buffy the Vampire Slayer*, have I got some stories for you. The FULL MOON books from St. Martin's Paperbacks are paranormal suspense novels featuring werewolf hunters. *Dark Moon* is available now and *Crescent Moon* will be out in early 2006.

Happy reading!

Lori Handeland

P.S. For information on future releases and a chance to win free books, visit my Web site at www.lorihandeland.com.

A SOLDIER'S QUEST
Lori Handeland

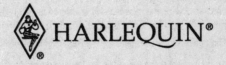

TORONTO • NEW YORK • LONDON
AMSTERDAM • PARIS • SYDNEY • HAMBURG
STOCKHOLM • ATHENS • TOKYO • MILAN • MADRID
PRAGUE • WARSAW • BUDAPEST • AUCKLAND

ISBN 0-373-71293-6

A SOLDIER'S QUEST

www.eHarlequin.com

Printed in U.S.A.

Books by Lori Handeland

HARLEQUIN SUPERROMANCE

*The Luchetti Brothers

For my editor, Johanna Raisanen

Smart, calm, articulate:
What more could a writer ask for?

PROLOGUE

BOBBY LUCHETTI RANG the doorbell at 445 Briar Lane. Holding his breath, he anticipated his first sight of Marlie Anderson.

Not that he didn't know what she looked like. He had a picture. One he'd kept in his wallet for more than two years now.

But he'd never seen her in person, never met the woman he'd fallen in love with by mail.

Had she moved on in the time he'd been missing? Had she met someone else and married him? Bobby hoped not, but he wouldn't blame her if she had.

A member of the elite Delta Force, Bobby had spent almost a year in Afghanistan traipsing from cave to cave in the hunt for Bin Laden. Done a bit of duty in Pakistan, too, ferreting out a cell of terrorists who were planning another attack on American soil.

He'd stopped writing Marlie when he received the orders for that mission. He hadn't thought it fair to keep her waiting when he wasn't sure if he'd return from Pakistan alive.

His gaze wandered over the two-story Colonial,

set on this quiet street in Minnesota. According to Marlie, hardly anything bad ever happened in Wind Lake.

The residents were like those of many small towns in America: traditionalists, old school, they took pride in who they were and where they came from. From Marlie's descriptions, Bobby had come to love Wind Lake as he loved her.

The door opened suddenly and Bobby stared at his brother, Colin. The resemblance between them was strong—dark hair, blue eyes, even their features. However, Colin was taller, slimmer, younger, and his hair was well past regulation length—but then so was Bobby's. Those in Delta Force were not required to cut their hair or shave or even wear a uniform, the better to blend in wherever they roamed.

The shock of seeing someone who didn't belong made Bobby blurt out, "What the hell are you doing here?"

Considering that Bobby had been listed as missing for quite a while, the question was one his brother should be asking him.

"You're alive," Colin said.

"Always have been."

"Do Mom and Dad know?"

"I called them as soon as I landed in the States."

"You didn't go home?"

"I had pressing business."

"More pressing than letting your mother know you aren't buried in a shallow grave?"

Bobby scowled. "She knows."

"You put her through hell, Bobby, and the rest of us, too."

"I got that when Mom took my head off by phone."

His family hadn't known until yesterday that Bobby was a member of Delta Force. Keeping such a secret wasn't unusual in the life of an operator, considering the dangerous nature of the job. Some of his men's wives only knew that their husbands did "something" for the army.

Bobby had thought what his loved ones didn't know wouldn't worry them; he couldn't have been more wrong.

"You knew I was alive," Bobby pointed out. "I rescued your sorry butt in Peshawar."

Typically, Colin had been unable to keep his nose out of other people's business—which was probably why he was a reporter. He'd followed a very thin trail to Pakistan and wound up getting himself kidnapped by a completely different set of terrorists than the one Bobby had infiltrated. The place was crawling with them.

They'd done their best to make Colin spill his guts. Luckily Bobby had managed to haul him out of there before the terrorists had figured out his brother was a worthless source of information.

"Last time I saw you, you were dressed…"

Colin let his gaze slide over Bobby's khaki trousers and crisp, blue shirt, a far cry from the robes and scarves he'd been sporting in Peshawar.

"Differently," Colin finished.

Bobby had only recently shaved his beard and removed the brown contacts that had disguised his foreign blue eyes. He should be more comfortable in American clothes, but he wasn't.

"That was over a year ago," Colin continued. "Not a phone call or even a letter. You're an asshole."

"I agree. But I'm very, very good at it."

Colin's mouth twitched. "I'm glad you're back. But why are you in Wind Lake?"

"If I learned one thing it's that I shouldn't waste time. I should tell people how I feel."

"What do you want to tell me?"

"Not you, moron. I've come to tell the woman I love that I love her."

His brother frowned. "What are you talking about?"

"Marlie. Is she here?" Bobby craned his neck, peering past Colin and into the house. "And why are you?"

Colin scrubbed a hand through his hair. "Bro, there's something you should know."

"Colin?" A woman's voice drifted from inside. "Who was at the door?"

Marlie appeared, fresh-faced, wholesome, with a baby on her hip and, from the appearance of her slightly rounded belly, another one on the way. Bobby just stared at her. Then he looked at his brother and understood.

"You son of a bitch."

"Bobby?" Marlie blinked. "When did you get back?"

Bobby ignored her. Colin was the one he was concerned with now.

"What part of 'take care of her' didn't you understand?"

"All of it," Colin said. "I thought you were friends. So did she."

In his head Bobby knew his brother was right. He hadn't been clear on what he wanted because he hadn't known himself. Until he'd spent countless months living in caves and tents.

He'd focused on Marlie's face, recalled every word she'd ever written to him. He'd made Wind Lake, Minnesota, the home he was fighting to protect and Marlie the woman worth risking his life for. Foolish, perhaps, when he'd never met her. Even more foolish, obviously, was sending his brother to watch over her.

Colin and Bobby had always been close. Colin should have been able to read between the lines of Bobby's cryptic note, which had been cryptic on purpose. He never knew when his mail was being intercepted and read by the enemy, or even a friend. One of the reasons he rarely wrote home.

He'd become nervous because he'd written Marlie so many times, tense that he was heading into the unknown and leaving her behind. The paranoia, which often kept him alive, grew and grew until he could think of little else but Marlie in Wind Lake, all innocent and alone. So he'd mailed Colin that note. And Colin had done exactly what he'd asked. He'd taken care of her.

Bobby's gaze fell to her swelling belly. More than once.

"This is Robbie." Marlie stepped forward, shifting the child in his direction. "We named him after you."

Bobby glanced at his brother, whose pale face had taken on a slightly greenish tinge. "Gee, thanks," he said.

"I—we—" Colin stared at Marlie helplessly.

It wasn't like Colin to be at a loss. He was a writer. He'd be in deep trouble if he couldn't find the words.

Marlie put her hand on Colin's arm. She wore a wedding ring. So did his brother. While that should make Bobby feel a bit better, at least the sneaky bastard had married her, he only felt worse. She was Colin's now, forever.

"Colin came here searching for you," she said. "And I fell in love with him. I couldn't help myself."

"Looks like he couldn't help himself, either."

She frowned. "He tried to stop what was happening between us, but I pointed out that you'd never said anything about love."

True. But that didn't mean he hadn't felt it.

"I wasn't sure if I'd come back."

Now she touched his arm, and he yearned for something that was never going to be. "I have to admit I had a little crush on you. But once I met Colin, those fantasies disappeared. I love him, Bobby. We were meant to be together."

Robbie started fussing, and Marlie withdrew her

hand to pat the squirming little boy. Bobby took a quick glance at the kid and found himself captured by bright blue Luchetti eyes. That child should be his.

His chest tightened and his stomach rolled. The dreams of a wife and a family had begun with her. The idea that someone was waiting for him, that a small part of him might be left if he was gone, had become a talisman. Bobby had sworn that if he got out of the Middle East in one piece, he'd make more of a life than what he had. That plan was as blown to hell as most of Afghanistan.

"I have to feed him," Marlie murmured. "You two should talk."

She disappeared inside.

"She's right." Colin stepped onto the porch and shut the door behind him. "We should talk."

"What's there to say? You married my girl and got her pregnant."

"That wasn't quite the order, but near enough."

Bobby went still. "You got her pregnant and *then* you married her?"

Colin flushed and rage burned through Bobby with a force that surprised him. He didn't even realize what he was going to do until his fist shot out and caught Colin on the chin.

His brother hit the ground like a sack of potatoes. Bobby didn't wait around to see if he'd knocked out any of Colin's teeth.

It wouldn't be the first time.

CHAPTER ONE

Two months later

SOMEDAY HIS TOMBSTONE might read: Another day, another hellhole.

And that would be fine with Bobby. He'd been in more down-and-out countries than he could remember. Most of the time no one even knew he was there before he was gone.

This mission, however, was different from the usual hit-and-run operation. He had a bad feeling this one might get him killed. Which would be an incredible joke on him.

"Mexico," he muttered. "No one dies in Mexico. Unless they drink the water."

Something skittered across the sand, then across Bobby's boot. The stench of rotting vegetation, or maybe just garbage, teased his nose. A baby cried; someone moaned. One dog's yip was answered by a dozen more. In Mexico, the ratio of stray dogs to drug dealers was about even.

Sweat trickled down his chest. In this heat a normal man would be wearing shorts instead of cargo pants, a muscle shirt instead of a black T-shirt, and sandals or bare feet instead of army boots.

Of course Bobby had never been normal—or so his brothers always told him.

"I could have been a farmer," he murmured.

But he'd chosen the army instead.

From his eighteenth year he'd worked his way up, until he was the elite of the elite. An operator, a D-boy, the Dreaded D—the army rarely uttered the word *Delta*—their force was that secret.

"So what am I doing here?"

Talking to himself, which he really needed to stop. Just because this was a cakewalk didn't mean he shouldn't follow procedure. Namely, no yapping in the jungle.

He'd come alone—singleton mission. Why waste two or more highly trained counterterrorism operators on an assignment that could be completed by a green recruit?

Though Delta's main function had once been hostage rescue, they'd become a lot more over the years. Bobby was now trained for threats on a global scale. Which was why it would be a genuine laugh-o-rama if he got killed rescuing the doctor daughter of a U.S. senator in the seemingly tame Yucatán Peninsula.

Of course, *tame* was a relative term. The state of Quintana Roo was a hotbed for drug cartels. Still, when compared to some of the places Bobby had been, some of the things he had seen, Mexico was downright peaceful. Nevertheless, even a docile dog could turn mean if poked too much and too hard.

Bobby pushed aside his misgivings, labeling the icy trickle of superstition down his spine as nothing more than another stream of sweat. He'd been living in sweaty countries for years. Why was the weather bothering him now?

Because he wanted this done. He wanted out of here. He wanted to go home.

And that was as strange as his premonition of disaster.

After leaving Wind Lake, Bobby had done what he did best. He disappeared. Not very adult of him, but he'd been upset, and he needed to return to the place where he was the strongest, the smartest, the best. When Bobby was in the field, he was the king and the world was his kingdom.

A short trip to Honduras had been followed by a longer one to Costa Rica. When the call had come in about the kidnapped doctor, he'd been so close it would have been foolish for him not to go.

Bobby shifted, lifting his night-vision goggles and taking yet another gander at the hut where Dr. Harker was supposedly detained. No moon tonight, but that didn't bother him. He could see pretty well in the dark, even without the goggles.

People milled around the last shack on the left; a few of them held submachine guns. There were too many souls in the vicinity to extract the good doctor without an outcry. He'd hang around until the majority went to bed, then disable the guards and slip away with the woman he'd been sent to rescue.

Having a plan made Bobby feel a whole lot better. He was spooked only because he missed home so badly. He never had before.

His mother, the queen of guilt, would have his head if she ever got hold of him. Shame tickled his gut. He'd called once after the fiasco with Colin, been thrilled when the answering machine picked up so he could leave a message telling everyone not to worry.

He hadn't called back because he didn't want to hear the lecture. Bobby would rather face…whatever…than listen to his mother when she was mad—and he had a feeling she was pretty mad right about now.

Bobby took another glance at the hut. The crowd had dispersed, leaving behind only the goons with guns. He'd give the village an hour to fall asleep, then he'd make his move.

Except the guards walked away. Not too far, but far enough that Bobby reconsidered disabling them. With a reasonable distraction, he could sneak into the hut and make off with the doctor. They might not know she was gone until morning, and by then it would be too late.

He tried to think of a diversion that wouldn't wake the entire village. Maybe a dog fight. If he could just find a nice piece of kibble, he'd throw it into the fray and—

A sudden stillness drew his attention. The men with the guns had disappeared. The doctor's hut stood quiet, dark, unguarded. This was too easy.

Did they know he was here? Were they setting a trap?

No way. If Bobby could do one thing extremely well, it was become invisible. Hell, he'd perfected that skill before he'd joined the army.

Growing up in a houseful of kids—five boys, one girl—with a mother who took nothing from no one and had eyes in the back of her head, Bobby had learned early on to sneak under the incredible radar of Eleanor Luchetti. A drug dealer with a submachine gun would run screaming if he spent more than two hours in the woman's company.

Bobby discovered he was smiling at the memory of his mommy and forced himself to stop. He was on a mission and he'd better get to it.

Needing to move quickly and silently, he concealed most of his equipment in the jungle. Taking only his sidearm, rifle and a knife in his boot, Bobby stuffed extra ammo in his voluminous and plentiful pant's pockets before creeping from his hiding place. He'd either make a clean getaway with the doctor, or return to his original plan, take out the guards, then get away with the doctor. With luck, he'd be home for dinner tomorrow.

He ran toward the hut, keeping low. The sand shifted beneath his boots with no more than a whisper. He reached the back of the shack and scanned the village.

Not an outcry was raised, not a shadow slunk anywhere that he could see. A dog barked, but with no more enthusiasm than before.

Success.

He peered into the hut through the hole in the

wall that served as a window. *"Psst,"* he whispered. "Doctor?"

The lump in the bed didn't move. Did he have the right place?

A more thorough examination of the interior revealed medical equipment and textbooks all jumbled together with girlie stuff on the table—although the girlie stuff in this case was sunscreen and a sturdy wide-brimmed hat with a red bandanna tied around the crown.

His sister, Kim, had always intermingled her lotions and potions with her schoolbooks, her hair ribbons with her pens and pencils. He didn't understand women. What a surprise.

Bobby slid past the curtain that doubled as a door. He opened his mouth to hail the doctor again, but the word stuck in his throat. The lump in the bed was gone.

"Shit," he muttered an instant before a knife pricked him in the side.

"Who are you?"

A tiny jab to the rock-solid back of the man who'd snuck into her quarters punctuated Jane's question.

"Dr. Harker?"

She frowned. American accent—upper Midwest from the sound of him. Big, bad, sneaky. Definitely military, but what was he doing in Quintana Roo?

"Who wants to know?"

"If you don't stop poking me with that thing, I'll be forced to take it away from you."

Jane snorted. She'd been down here long enough to learn a few things about knives and self-defense.

The next instant he was holding the knife and she was holding her stinging wrist. Maybe she wasn't as smart as she thought she was. And wasn't that just the story of her life?

Her gaze drifted over his weapons—a pistol and a rifle, in addition to her knife. Jane didn't know much about guns, except that they made nasty, gaping holes in people she was often forced to fix. She hated firearms, and the men who wielded them.

"You *are* Dr. Harker?" he pressed.

Jane shrugged, nodded. If he was going to kill her, he was going to kill her, regardless of who she was. She'd seen his face.

A very nice face beneath several days' growth of dark beard—handsome if you went for Clint Eastwood before too many years in the sun and the wind had taken their toll. She didn't—but that didn't mean she couldn't appreciate good-looking when she saw it.

Blue eyes, nearly black hair, which was a lot longer than she'd ever seen on a soldier. He was taller than her but not by much. At five-foot-eleven inches, Jane towered over most men of her acquaintance. She didn't like it any better than they did, but what choice did she have?

Muscles bulged against the dark shirt. She hoped he had more than muscle between his ears, but she doubted it. In her expert medical opinion, overachieving in one area usually meant underachievement in another.

Huge muscles, small brain. Big gun, itsy-bitsy male equipment.

The urge to laugh was nearly overwhelming. Why she was always consumed with mirth at the most inopportune times Jane had never been able to figure out.

"Take what you need," he snapped. "We have to get out of here before the guards return."

"I'm not going anywhere."

"I don't have time to argue, ma'am— I mean, Doctor. For some reason the guards wandered off, but they'll be back." He glanced out the door. "I'd rather not kill them if I don't have to."

Kill Juan and Enrique? Not while Jane was alive and kicking.

"Listen, soldier boy, there'll be no killing. There's been enough."

"Works for me. Let's go."

Grabbing her arm, he tugged her along. Jane dug in and tried to stand her ground. But he was huge and all she succeeded in doing was stumbling into him, where she discovered he was as hard and strong as he appeared. She shoved at his solid chest, and wonder of wonders, he let her go.

"What do you need?" Bouncing on the tips of his toes, he was action man, ready for anything.

"I need sleep. Go away."

"I'm here to rescue you."

"From what? The fleas?"

"You've been kidnapped. You're being held for ransom by drug dealers."

She choked back another laugh. "Since when?"

"How the hell should I know? I'm just following orders."

"What orders?" Her laughter faded. "Who are you?"

"Captain Luchetti. U.S. Special Forces."

Jane lifted a brow. *Special Forces?* Either this was serious, or he was nuts. Which would be a damn shame because, aside from the mistake he'd made in coming here, he seemed to be pretty good at this.

"I haven't been kidnapped. I've been working here for over a year."

"But— Your mother—"

Jane cursed. Her mother. Of course.

She'd been bugging Jane to quit her job with Doctors of Mercy—an international, nonprofit association that sent doctors to underprivileged areas of the world—since she'd taken it. But Jane couldn't believe her mother would lie, then take advantage of her position as a U.S. senator to send a very expensively trained soldier to drag Jane home. If word of this got out, the scandal just might ruin the senator's career. And wouldn't that be a shame?

Jane stifled a smirk, then stared Luchetti up and down. She might not be much for beefcake—Jane preferred scholarly men, tall blondes with wire-rimmed glasses and slim, artist's hands—but soldier boy really was nice to look at.

Poor man. This trip had been a colossal waste of his time.

"There's been a misunderstanding," she began. "I'm not—"

"Whatever," he said shortly. "You can explain it in Washington."

"What? No. I'm not leaving. I've got work to do."

"My orders are to bring you back. Period."

"And you always follow orders?"

He didn't bother to answer what to him had to be a stupid question. Of course he always followed orders. If he didn't he wouldn't be what he was.

"I want to talk to your superior."

"Me, too," he muttered.

"Well…?"

"Interception of information by satellite, radio and cell phones is a lot easier than you think."

"Which means?"

"No contact until we get to the airfield."

"What airfield?"

"Halfway between here and Puerto."

"You can't be serious!"

Puerto was nearly forty miles through the jungle.

He winced. "Keep it down, will you? You want your kidnappers to hear us?"

"I have *not* been kidnapped. Or at least not yet. If you drag me into the jungle, *that's* kidnapping."

He rolled his eyes and managed to appear bored even when his body was as tense as a hound dog on a leash and his toe had started tapping against the dirt floor of her hut in an annoyingly staccato rhythm. Little puffs of dust rose and sullied what had once undoubtedly been shiny black boots.

Why didn't he just tape a neon sign to his back that said *U.S. Army Top Secret Soldier?* Even without the pistol at his waist and the rifle slung across his chest, he'd hardly fit in around here.

"The Doctors of Mercy sent me to help the people of this village," Jane explained. "The guards are for my protection."

"Uh-huh. That's why they wandered into the trees for a smoke or a leak."

"Well, there isn't much to protect me from."

"You're going to tell me you haven't seen any drug dealers around here?"

Jane went silent. There were drug dealers all over the place. She'd taken bullets out of quite a few of them, sewn up gashes and punctures, even treated overdoses. But she didn't ask questions. That was the quickest road to an unmarked grave in the jungle.

"I thought so," he murmured when she didn't answer.

"Why would I lie about being kidnapped?"

"I don't know, why would you?"

Jane stifled the urge to shriek in frustration. It wouldn't do any good.

"I am *not* lying. I'm fine. Not a care in the world, so…thanks for stopping by. Nice meeting you."

Jane had only taken a single step toward her bunk when he grabbed her by the elbow and yanked her right back.

"I told you before, my orders are to bring you home. If the information was FUBAR, that isn't my problem."

"FUBAR?" she asked, but he wasn't listening.

Instead, he cocked his head and whispered, *"Shh."*

Jane opened her mouth to call out to Juan and Enrique. Captain Luchetti slapped his big, hard hand over her lips.

Indignant, at first she didn't hear the conversation, then she didn't understand it. And not because the men approaching her hut were speaking Spanish—she'd taken the language all through high school and college—but because what they were saying did not compute.

Something about burying her in the soft silt near the river.

BOBBY KEPT HIS HAND over Dr. Harker's face and tried to make sense of the words. His Arabic was impeccable; his Spanish far from it. Nevertheless, he'd been in enough Hispanic countries and around enough Hispanic soldiers to get the gist, even before he caught the doctor's name and felt her go rigid in his arms.

He glanced out the small hole in the curtain that passed for a door. Her guards were back. *Damn.* Why hadn't he thrown her over his shoulder and gotten out while the getting was good?

He'd been taught how to rescue POWs, had even gone through SERE—Survival, Evasion, Resistance, Escape—training to be prepared should he be detained and interrogated.

Prisoners were often terrified of their captors and

might behave in one of two ways—by turning on them after liberation and tearing them to pieces, or by being so afraid of retaliation they were unable to leave their prison at all.

Dr. Harker wasn't behaving in the usual way—of course, she hadn't been kidnapped—still, Bobby should have followed instructions and removed her by *any* means necessary.

"Matele."

Double damn. That word he knew. *Kill* in any language had a certain ring to it.

He turned the doctor to face him, indicating by an urgent finger to the lips that she should be quiet. Then he hurried to the cot, placed her pillow beneath the sheet, snatched the folded blanket from the foot of the bed and hustled back.

In the shadowy corner of the hut, Bobby shoved her under a table, fluffed the blanket over top, then crawled in after, tugging the end to the floor and leaving a slit of space near the leg so he could see out.

Not a second too soon. One of the goons strode in. He didn't look to the left or the right, didn't pause until he stood directly next to the cot. Bobby knew what was coming next, and he covered the doctor's mouth again.

Two muffled shots. Silencer. Double tap to the head.

Dr. Harker jerked with each sound, but she didn't cry out and she didn't faint. Nevertheless, he kept his hand over her lips until the assassin exited the room.

Bobby could have dispatched the would-be murderer with ease, but then the guy's friends would have come searching for him, and there'd have been more dispatching, more bodies. Definitely not worth the trouble.

Luckily the killer was both a coward and an idiot. He hadn't checked to see if his victim was dead. He hadn't checked to see if she was even there at all.

"He thinks he killed you," Bobby breathed into Dr. Harker's ear.

She nodded, and he lowered his hand from her face. She turned, and he was struck by a sense of fragility, which was downright odd considering the doctor was far from small and impressively fierce.

She wasn't pretty—not that such things mattered. He'd learned long ago that the loveliest faces often hid the ugliest souls.

Her hair was an indistinct color, between brown and blond; her braid brushed her waist. Shock and fear made her eyes appear huge in her suddenly pale face.

She'd come after him with a knife. He should have been angry, instead he'd been intrigued.

Bobby shook his head. Now was not the time to get distracted. He needed to figure out why he'd been sent here to rescue her from nothing.

His gaze drifted over the place where she would have been sleeping. Maybe he hadn't been rescuing her from nothing after all.

But why had the senator called in every favor she was owed to send Bobby to Mexico to save her daughter *before* she'd needed saving?

And then there was the matter of semantics. Murder versus kidnapping. Equally unpleasant but not interchangeable, even in Spanish.

Something strange was going on, but Bobby didn't have the time or the inclination to unravel the mystery at the moment.

"You ready to go?"

Her only answer was a nod.

CHAPTER TWO

ENRIQUE HAD TRIED to kill her. Jane couldn't get her mind around that fact.

The man who'd laughed with her, eaten with her, taken care of her when she was ill with the Mexican version of the twenty-four-hour flu had coolly walked into her hut and put two bullets into her brain.

That her brain had not been where he thought it was at the time did not excuse him in the least.

Luchetti climbed out from under the table and reached back. Dazed, Jane put her hand into his.

His skin was even hotter than the tropical climate. Though nearly the same height, he probably outweighed her by fifty pounds of pure muscle. From the appearance of his biceps, he could bench press a donkey without breaking a sweat. Touching him should be unpleasant, but it wasn't.

She pushed aside the disturbing thought. There was no way she was attracted to a Neanderthal like him. Captain Luchetti's very existence went against everything she'd ever believed in.

Jane didn't approve of war; she loathed violence

and she specifically detested big, muscle-bound men who radiated testosterone like a foul odor. Too bad Luchetti was all that stood between her and more violence than she'd ever encountered in her thirty years on earth.

He glanced out the window of her hut. "They're gone. So are we."

"But—"

"*Now*, Doctor, before one of them grows a brain."

Jane's gaze flitted over her books, her instruments, her medical supplies. He saw what she was looking at and shook his head. "Maybe someone who doesn't want you dead can ship everything to you later."

She wouldn't need it shipped because she'd be back. Just like Arnold Schwarzenegger but with less fanfare. All she'd ever wanted to do was help the helpless. Now she was one of them. Jane didn't care for the feeling.

"Do you have any food or water in here?" Luchetti used one finger to lift the corner of a blanket, another to move aside a text on preventative medicine for the tropics.

Jane nodded and reached under her bed for the few bottles of tepid water. She averted her eyes from the bullet holes in her pillow. The very thought of them made her sick.

She turned and nearly jumped out of her skin. Luchetti was so close she could feel the heat steaming off of him. Why was he so hot?

Her cheeks flushed at the double meaning. What

was wrong with her? She'd been in danger before, and she'd never wanted to jump the bones of the nearest male. Until today.

She needed to curb that impulse before she embarrassed herself. A guy like Luchetti would never be interested in a woman like her.

He lifted his arm. Her backpack hung from his hand. The same backpack she'd used through both college and medical school at Harvard. The bag had been good luck then, maybe there was a little luck left.

Quickly Jane tossed the water and the few supplies she kept for emergencies—juice boxes, crackers, animal cookies—as well as a mini first-aid kit into the sack.

Luchetti motioned for her to follow. "Stay close," he murmured, and slid out the door.

Jane stayed so close she stepped on the back of his boots more than once. To his credit, he never said a word, never made a single sound of irritation.

The sky was dark, the stars fading. Soon dawn would tint the horizon. She hoped they were far away from here before then.

A *woof* from the other side of the village reminded Jane of certain responsibilities. Snapping her fingers, she gave a low whistle. But many of the dogs were out chasing prey, including the one that had come with her hut.

Luchetti shot her a glare, and she opened her mouth to ask what she'd done that was so terrible. Then she remembered.

She was supposed to be dead.

Captain Luchetti entered the lush, overgrown vegetation and seemed to disappear. Jane blinked, tilted her head, squinted. Had she dreamed the entire incident? She'd give a year's salary—not much, but all she had—if she could wake up on her own pillow, minus two bullet holes, with the sun shining in her face and one of the villagers calling her name.

Logically Jane realized she was in shock, with a roaring case of denial. Even so, she stared at the place where Luchetti had gone until his hand reached out and yanked her in after him.

"What are you doing?" he growled.

The jungle closed around her—the buzz of the insects, the trill of the birds, the smell of wet foliage turning to rot. The air was heavy with heat and the night. She tried to see his face, but she couldn't.

Panic threatened, and Jane took a single step back. Who was this man really? He'd said he was Special Forces, but maybe he wasn't. Maybe he meant to take her into the wilderness and dump her where no one would ever find her.

Luchetti still held Jane's arm, and when she inched farther away, his grip tightened. "We don't have much time, Doctor. I'd prefer not to leave a trail of dead people, but I will if I have to."

"Wh-what?" Her voice shook and she cursed the weakness.

She was an adult, a respected member of the medical community and the daughter of a senator. She *would not* be afraid. Or at least she wouldn't show it.

His sigh dripped with impatience. "If they come after you, I'll kill them."

Plain. Simple. To the point. She didn't have to see his face or look into his eyes to know he was telling the truth.

This man might be more dangerous than the ones he was protecting her from. Captain Luchetti could break her neck with his hands. Shoot first and ask questions later. Mow down the village, bury the bodies and have the government cover for him. It had happened before.

"D-do you have any identification?"

His answer was a snort.

"You say you're Special Forces, but how do I know that for certain?"

"You don't. Come with me or take your chances with the drug-dealing scum."

Under any other circumstances Jane would have laughed at his words. He sounded like a commando in a low-budget war flick.

Jane frowned and glanced uneasily around the jungle. Could she be a victim of a new reality show? *Punked in Mexico. Survivor: the Rescue. American Kidnapping.*

Her denial was moving rapidly toward paranoia.

"If I have to, I'll carry you out of here," Luchetti murmured. "But it'll be a lot easier on both of us if I don't have to."

"Why didn't you bring a helicopter?"

As they whispered back and forth he shoved at the ground cover with his boot. "I might not be a doctor, Doctor, but I have rescued a hostage or two."

"I wasn't a hostage."

"I didn't know that." Leaning over, he moved aside the thick fronds with his hands. "The quickest way to get someone killed is to hover a helo over the area. Psycho murderers tend to get trigger-happy with all that noise and light."

He probably had a point.

Suddenly he cursed and dropped to his knees, digging through the foliage.

"What's the matter?" Jane asked.

"My stuff is gone."

"When you say 'stuff,' you mean—"

"Satellite phone, night-vision goggles, various demolition items." He sat back on his heels.

"Did they get your decoder ring and your bat utility belt, too?"

She couldn't see his face, but she felt his scowl. "Don't be a wise guy. I need those things."

"Hold on," Jane said. "What happened to 'no contact until we reached the air field'?"

"There isn't."

"Yet you had a satellite phone?"

"In case of emergency." He stood and took hold of her arm again. "Like now."

"What emergency?"

Luchetti leaned in close. His breath brushed her forehead; his heat swept over her skin and Jane shivered. What was it about this man that both attracted and repelled her?

"Someone either knows I'm here or—"

He broke off and lifted his gaze to the sky.

"Or?" she prompted.

"Or they will know as soon as they get a peek at the prime American gear they just stole."

"Nice job, Rambo."

"Yeah." With a sigh of disgust, he lowered his head. "I thought you'd like that."

THEY WERE BEING FOLLOWED.

Bobby cursed the loss of his equipment. He could really use a few of those items right now.

He couldn't figure out how everything could have disappeared so fast unless someone had been following him. And if they'd been following him, why not shoot him instead of just stealing his toys? There were more mysteries to this mission than answers.

At least he had his Browning .45 and the sniper rifle designed especially for Delta. Gun manufacturers just loved to create weapons for America's elite force, even if they couldn't advertise that they'd done so. Nevertheless, most Delta operators stuck with the tried-and-true Browning instead of newer and fancier models.

Glancing over his shoulder, Bobby saw nothing out of the ordinary. Whoever was following them was good, but Bobby was better.

Even though he'd come to Mexico in a hurry, he'd come prepared. During the plane ride he'd pored over maps, plotted his strategy and their escape. He knew this area as well as it was possible for him to know it on paper. Though he mourned the lack of proper reconnaissance, Bobby had learned in fifteen years of army living that he couldn't have everything.

He should count himself lucky to have a map, water, food and Dr. Harker, alive.

Still, what he wouldn't give to have one of the army's elite Night Stalker pilots on alert. The 160th SOAR was responsible for chauffeuring Delta into some of the most dangerous areas in the world. Quintana Roo would be easy. Sadly, sending Bobby was all that had been warranted for this mission. He'd have to do without the superior air support.

He glanced at the doctor. "You doin' okay?"

"I'm fine." Her voice was clipped, annoyed. He couldn't blame her. He'd be mighty pissed off if someone tried to shoot him in his sleep.

Not that it hadn't happened. More times than he cared to count. But the people who tried to kill Bobby did so because if they didn't, he'd kill them first. He had no idea what her bodyguard's excuse was.

Bobby kept walking, shoving his way through the dense underbrush. A quick glance at his compass revealed they were on track—at least for now.

His life was another matter. For the last couple of years he'd felt at odds. Happy in the job he'd always wanted, yet lonely despite living, for the most part, with dozens of men.

Easing that loneliness with one-night sexual encounters had become more sad than fun. He'd only found one woman he was interested in spending his life with, and she was married to his brother.

Bobby thrust the depressing thoughts away. They'd been creeping up on him too often lately. He'd say he was getting old, except thirty-three was far from it. Still, life in the Special Forces made men age faster than most.

He'd seen things that would give other people nightmares forever. He'd done things for which there was no forgiveness. Yet he had no regrets. He'd become the man he'd always wanted to be. So why wasn't he happy?

"How much farther?" Dr. Harker asked.

"Few hours."

She sighed but didn't complain.

An odd sound made him stop and listen intently. Had that been a bird or a man, a dog or a monkey?

"What is it?"

He glanced at the doctor. Should he tell her they were being followed or keep it to himself?

"How far away are they?" she asked.

He lifted his brows. She continued to surprise him.

"Far enough."

"*Who* are they?"

"You tell me."

"I have no idea. I didn't even know I was kidnapped."

He stifled a smile. He shouldn't like her so much.

In a few hours he'd never see Dr. Harker again. In a few weeks she'd forget she'd ever met him. Which was as it should be.

Another hour passed. Whoever was following them must be part wolf because, despite a tempo he hadn't reached since Special Ops selection, he and the doctor weren't getting ahead. Bobby couldn't figure it out.

She was keeping up, but she was fading. The increasing heat of the day didn't help.

"Do you jog?" he asked.

Dr. Harker blew a bead of sweat from her nose with an irritated puff of her lips. "You want to *jog?*"

"No." He glanced at the trail behind them and frowned. Or at least not yet.

Bobby returned his attention to the doctor. "Just wondering why you're in such great shape."

"I walk. A lot."

"Walk?"

"Yeah, put one foot in front of the other? You remember it. From before you were a soldier boy."

She surprised a laugh out of him. His mother and sister were the sarcasm twins, his brother Dean, the king. Bobby usually refrained from playing since he couldn't compete, but he'd always found dry humor amusing.

"Keep on keeping on, Luchetti." She waved a hand. "I'll be right there with you."

A sudden burst of sound from behind them and Bobby reacted, spinning with gun in hand. Something erupted from the foliage—something low to the ground and hairy, running straight at the doctor.

He leveled the pistol, but before he could fire, Dr. Harker launched herself at him. "No!"

Bobby pulled up. The doctor tripped over a rock and fell down. He tried to catch her, but he only had one free hand, and he missed.

She hit the dirt with a thud and a grunt. The furry thing pounced on top of her. He wasn't sure, but he thought it was a dog.

"Don't shoot," the doctor cried. "She's mine."

Bobby had been raised on a farm. He'd seen all sorts of domestic animals. His dad kept Dalmatians. Now, those were dogs.

This…that…it? Hell. What?

The animal licking Dr. Harker's arm, neck and cheek appeared to be a starving coyote crossed with a hairless cat. The beast was stick thin. Her fur was an indeterminate color—gray, brown, a little black and white—with patches of pink skin like polka dots across her bony butt.

When she lifted her head, Bobby blinked. The creature had only one eye. He took a step forward, planning to pull the flea-bitten mutt off his charge, and the beast snarled at him. She was short a few teeth, too, though there were enough left to do some damage.

Bobby pointed the gun and narrowed his eyes.

"Down, girl," Dr. Harker said.

The dog stepped daintily off the doctor's back and sat at her side.

Dr. Harker indicated Bobby's weapon. "Put that away."

He did, but he could have sworn the animal was laughing at him. Her tongue lolled as she panted louder than a freight train.

"What is it?" he asked.

"You've never seen a dog?"

"That isn't a dog."

The doctor frowned. "You'll hurt her feelings. Lucky thinks she's beautiful."

"Lucky hasn't looked in the mirror lately." Bobby contemplated the one-eyed mangy mutt. "Why on earth would you name *that* Lucky?"

"Because I was lucky to find her. She's a good girl. Aren't you, sweetie?"

The dog turned and licked the doctor from chin to forehead. Bobby winced. Lord knew where that mouth had been.

"Unsanitary much?" he muttered.

Her glance was filled with surprise. "Dogs are much cleaner than humans. I'd rather kiss a dog any day."

He wasn't sure what to say to that except, "Send her back where she came from."

"She's with me."

"I don't think so."

"Lucky followed me this far. She gets an all-expense-paid trip to America."

"You didn't say anything about a pet."

"You didn't ask me." At his scowl, she hurried on. "Lucky comes and goes. I knew we couldn't search for her. But if I don't take her with me, she'll die. There are far too many dogs in Mexico, and Lucky isn't exactly a beauty queen. No one will take her in."

"I can't traipse through the jungle with…that. What about the guys following us?"

"Maybe Lucky was following us."

Bobby went silent. She might be right. Then again, she might not be.

"Lucky's the best watchdog in the village," the doctor continued.

"She did a bang-up job last night."

"She wasn't there last night."

Bobby sighed. "You can't expect me to show up at the airfield with—" He broke off.

He couldn't call her a dog, that wouldn't be fair to dogs.

Dr. Harker narrowed her eyes. "What's the difference? I'm sure the plane has plenty of room."

Not nearly enough if he had to share space with Lucky, the ugliest mutt in the world.

"She'll only follow us," Dr. Harker wheedled. "You may as well let her stay."

Bobby threw up his hands. "Fine. Whatever. Why don't you bring all of the stray dogs back with you?"

She contemplated him with a deadpan expression. "Now, that would just be foolish."

JANE KEPT AN ARM around Lucky. There was no way she was leaving the dog behind. Lucky loved Jane more than anyone else ever had.

Only Luchetti's ferocious scowl kept her from grinning with joy at Lucky's presence. She never would have pegged him for an animal hater.

"Come on." He offered his hand.

Lucky growled.

"Relax, girl," Jane murmured, and the dog went silent.

She would have preferred to get up under her own power, but she was exhausted. She might walk a lot, but she'd never walked this long at a stretch.

Jane allowed Luchetti to haul her upright. Pain rocketed up her right ankle and seemed to settle at the base of her spine. She stumbled into his arms.

"What's the matter?"

"I must have twisted my ankle when I fell."

"You're kidding."

"Not this time."

His lips tightened. Only then did she notice what a nice mouth he had—full and wide. He should smile more.

Of course he probably saw little in this world to smile about. The same could be said for Jane, although the children she treated gave her a good laugh every day. If not for them, she might get caught up in all the misery—like Captain Luchetti had.

"You'll have to piggyback."

"I beg your pardon?"

He turned around and bent his knees. "Climb on. I'll carry you."

"You can't. I'm a lot heavier than I look."

"And I'm a lot less patient than I act. Get on."

Less patient? His fuse was the shortest she'd ever known. Maybe he was teasing, but she couldn't really tell.

"I'm sure if I bind the ankle I can walk."

"We don't have time, Doctor."

She hesitated for another few seconds, then gave in to the inevitable and climbed onto his back. Luchetti trotted down the trail at an impressive clip, though still slower than the pace they'd traveled together. Lucky woofed once and followed.

"Where are you from that you don't know what a piggyback is?" he asked.

"I know. I just didn't believe you could carry me."

He laughed. "I've carried two-hundred-and-fifty-pound men over my shoulder, with bullets flying and people dying."

"Well, hoo-ah," she muttered, using the gung-ho army expression for let's go, get 'em and so forth.

"You aren't impressed?" he asked.

She was, but she wasn't going to let him know it.

"Where are you from that you don't like dogs?" she countered.

"I like dogs fine."

"You weren't very nice to Lucky."

"That isn't a dog," he repeated.

She let her left foot bang against his thigh, hard.

"Watch it," he muttered, and she smirked.

Lucky followed in Luchetti's footsteps, prancing like a French poodle. The dog made Jane smile. Lucky wasn't pretty, but she thought she was—or maybe she just didn't care. Pretty didn't feed you. Pretty didn't save you from the vultures, but attitude could. Lucky had attitude times three. Jane wished she could be half as confident.

Seeing Jane glance her way, the dog mumbled and grumbled in her own peculiar manner.

"What was that?" Luchetti snapped.

"Lucky. She talks."

"Sounded like a dying cow."

"You've heard a lot of dying cows, have you?"

"My fair share."

"Oh, really. Where was that?"

"Illinois."

"There's a huge need for Special Forces in Illinois?"

"You know we can't operate in the U.S."

"I do?"

"Posse Comitatus Act ring any bells?"

Actually, it did, thanks to her mother's habit of discussing business at the dinner table.

Federal soldiers were prohibited from operating as law-enforcement officers inside the Unites States—unless the act was temporarily suspended by the president.

"So you're from Illinois?"

"Dairy farm near Bloomington."

"Never been there."

"You didn't miss much."

Jane frowned. Most people pined for home while they were away. Luchetti had no doubt been posted to some mighty unpleasant places. By now Illinois should look great. She had to wonder why it didn't.

Jane was tempted to ask more, nevertheless she kept silent. She was very good with patients, spent most of her time examining people and discussing private matters. Maybe that was why she'd never been any good at getting personal in social situations.

Pretty sad when bouncing along piggyback through the dense Mexican underbrush was the biggest social event she'd had in years.

CHAPTER THREE

JANE HAD DEVOTED her life to helping others. She had no time for men and little interest in marriage. She'd seen enough of her colleagues dragged down by love—or what they thought was love. Brilliant women with a stellar career in front of them, giving it all up because hubby wanted them home.

Gag. True love meant support, not criticism. Encouragement, not censure. She'd never met a man who could keep his mouth shut and let his wife shine. Not even her father.

Jane pushed thoughts of dead old dad out of her mind. He'd walked out when she was a child. By the time he'd passed away, she hadn't seen or heard from him in fifteen years. That kind of love she didn't need.

But a little affection would be nice. Not that she hadn't had boyfriends.

Well, not boyfriends, exactly.

Lovers?

Maybe that wasn't the right word either, since love had never been mentioned.

Jane wasn't the type of woman to inspire pretty

words and everlasting devotion. She'd come to terms with that long ago.

If not boyfriends or lovers, what should she call them? Guys she'd had sex with sounded so crass.

She'd enjoyed the social company of men, slept with a few, then sent them on their way before they could send her. Thus far she'd never missed a single one for more than a minute. Which left a certain dilemma.

Jane wanted children. They were the one pure thing in an impure world. What wasn't to like? Kids adored Jane, and she adored them right back. However, as her mother often reminded her, she'd have to be more than social with a man to get one.

Jane didn't mind being social, she didn't even mind the sex, but what she really wanted was the child without the husband.

Her mother had nearly had an apoplectic fit when Jane had voiced that opinion in front of a cardinal and a senior senator from Mississippi.

Poor Mother. She enjoyed introducing her daughter, the doctor. But then Jane would open her mouth, start talking about AIDS and pestilence and the starving children in Somalia, and Raeanne Harker's joy would turn to distaste. Jane really had to stop having so much fun at her mother's expense.

Except she couldn't count how many big, fat checks were slipped into her hand after Raeanne had swept out of the room in a snit.

"Like taking candy from a baby," she murmured. "What baby?"

Oops.

Talking to herself again, a common occurrence in the village, since no one had spoken much English.

"Never mind," Jane said. "I can walk now."

Luchetti kept jogging so she tapped him on the head with her knuckle. "Hey, pal, put me down."

He stopped, she thought to do as she asked. Instead, he tilted his head, swiveled around and murmured, *"Shh."*

Lucky growled, low and vicious—the sound she saved for the most dangerous predators.

"Drug dealer," Jane whispered.

Luchetti shot an incredulous look over his shoulder, and Jane shrugged. "Seriously."

Lucky *hated* drug dealers and made her feelings known whenever one was in the vicinity. Jane figured the dog could smell the product on their skin—it was the only explanation. At any rate, Lucky was doing her drug-dealer snarl louder than Jane had ever heard before.

Outcries erupted in Spanish. Feet pounded down the trail, and a gunshot sounded an instant before something whizzed by Jane's right ear.

Luchetti complied with Jane's earlier demand by dumping her into the vegetation. She broke her fall with her hands and a shaft of pain made her wince. But with bullets flying overhead there was no time for concern over broken bones or torn ligaments.

"Stay down," Luchetti said urgently.

An unnecessary demand, since Jane was already pressed as close to the ground as she could get.

Lucky, who'd been set to tear off a piece of some-one, now cowered next to Jane, pretending to be Flat Dog, relative of Gumby.

Luchetti yanked his rifle clear of the sling across his chest and started firing. A sharp outcry soon fol-lowed.

"Got one." He grinned.

"You don't have to be so happy about it."

He didn't even glance her way, keeping his sharp blue eyes trained on the area the bullets hailed from. "They're trying to kill us, Doctor. I'm not going to feel bad about doing the same."

"Isn't there another way? Talk to them? Offer money? Something."

"If they think we have money, they'll kill us for sure. The only thing men like these understand is force that's greater than theirs."

"But we don't have force that's greater than theirs."

"Speak for yourself. One American soldier is a match for ten of those guys."

"Hoo-ah," she muttered again, but he ignored her.

The bullets flew, and Jane began to worry about am-munition. Luchetti kept yanking shells from the pock-ets of his pants, but that wasn't going to last forever.

He never fired indiscriminately, but waited and watched before shooting. Nearly every time he pulled the trigger, someone fell.

At last, when they'd been pinned down for nearly an hour, the shooting slowed, then stopped alto-gether. Lucky gave a low *woof.*

Jane quickly covered the dog's muzzle with her hand, but no more bullets came blasting through the trees. "They must have left."

"Or they want us to think they did, then lift our heads to look so they can blow them off."

"Or that."

Luchetti gave a cough that sounded suspiciously like a laugh. Did he think she was funny? Hardly anyone ever did. Jane might like him for that alone—even without the stunning blue eyes and great big biceps.

"Now what do we do?" she asked.

"I'd like to circle around, make sure they're gone."

"But?"

"I can't leave you alone."

Jane rolled her eyes. "I can take care of myself, soldier boy."

"Right."

"Stop humoring me. Go see if the bad guys fled before your military might. We'll be all right."

He hesitated.

"Or we could keep hiding behind the bushes until we're old."

"Fine." He jerked his pistol from the holster and held the weapon out to her, butt first.

Jane made a face. "No thanks, I'm trying to cut down."

"Hardy-har-har. Take it."

"No."

"Then we'll sit here until we're old."

Jane narrowed her eyes. Luchetti tightened his lips. She knew that expression of bullheaded stubbornness. She recognized it from the mirror.

"Give me that." Jane took the pistol with two fingers and set it on the ground with the muzzle facing away from her.

"Do you know how to fire a gun?"

"I know how to remove a bullet from a body, I think I can figure it out."

The captain sighed and picked up the weapon again. "This gun is a little tricky." He aimed the pistol toward the trees. Lucky whimpered and hit the dirt. He cast her a quick, concerned glance. "That dog gun shy?"

"No, she's smart. Guns kill people, and their little dogs, too."

"*People* kill people."

"Blah, blah, blah. Spare me the NRA propaganda and get on with it."

Luchetti shrugged. "Point the long end at a bad guy. Pull back the hammer, then squeeze the trigger. Keep squeezing it until you're out of bullets or bad guys. Got it?"

"I think so." Luchetti handed Jane the gun, and she set the weapon back on the ground.

He rubbed his forehead as if an ache had started in the center. "If someone attacks, you won't have time to pick that up, thumb the hammer and fire."

Since Jane wasn't sure she'd be able to shoot anyone, anyway, she didn't mind. But he started to get that stubborn expression again, so she took the gun and held it tightly in her hand.

"You're left-handed?"

Jane nodded.

"Huh. So's my brother."

Before she could comment, he melted into the trees.

Lucky watched him go with her tongue hanging out. Jane had to agree with the sentiment.

"So soldier boy has a brother, and here I thought they grew him in a lab."

Jane waited and listened. Lucky panted faster; Jane prayed harder. No guns were fired; no outcry was raised. But that didn't mean the bad guys had gone. However, Lucky had stopped snarling. Jane trusted the dog's instincts more than anyone's.

Time seemed to slow. The silence after so much noise was oppressive. Jane's fingers clenched the grip of the weapon until they ached.

When the foliage rustled behind her, she gasped and swung in that direction.

Luchetti raised a brow. "For a pacifist you took to the gun awful fast."

"Who said I was a pacifist?"

"I can smell bleeding-heart liberals a mile away."

Jane scowled as she put the firearm back on the ground. "Probably because they smell a lot sweeter than war-mongering soldier boys."

"Probably."

He let her rudeness bounce off him like a Nerf basketball. Which only made Jane feel small, nasty and ungrateful.

"I apologize."

He shrugged. "I've heard worse—in ten languages."

He no doubt had, which only made her feel smaller, nastier and less grateful.

"They're gone," he continued.

"How many...?" Jane wasn't sure how to ask for the number of men he'd killed. Was that an appropriate question?

"Six. Two headed back the way we came. I doubt we'll see them again."

The cockiness was understandable considering his skill at the job. Nevertheless...

"*Why* won't we see them again?"

"We didn't see them this time."

Well, that was comforting.

"We're nearly to the airfield. They won't come any closer to an American base."

"We have a base in Mexico? Since when?"

"Not a base, base." He took a deep breath. "Never mind."

"Top-secret, double-naught spy stuff?"

"I'm not a spy," he said quickly.

"What, exactly, are you?"

"Special Forces."

"You already said that. Which kind?"

"The secret kind."

She searched her memory. There was only one area of the special forces where the operatives were removed from the data banks of the U.S. Army.

"Delta." Jane's eyes bugged. "You're *Delta?*"

"*Shh.* You want the whole world to know?"

"Delta Force is some hotshot antiterrorist unit—"

"*Counter*terrorist."

"What?"

"We respond to terrorist acts—*after* they happen."

"Sure you do."

He could tell her all day that Delta didn't take out terrorists before they blew people up. She wasn't going to believe him.

His face went mulish at the heavy dose of skepticism in her voice and she hurried on. "The point is, what are you doing here?"

"Exactly what I was thinking."

Jane bit her lip. Her mother was going to be in deep doo-doo if it ever got out that she'd sent a Delta Force operator to rescue a daughter who didn't need rescuing.

Well, maybe she had needed a *little* rescuing. But…Delta?

That was like sending a shark after a guppy, dropping an atomic bomb on a riot.

Jane sighed. Like sending a superhero after Plain Jane of the Yucatán.

BOBBY WAS SQUIRRELLY, and he couldn't figure out why. He'd routed the evil drug lords and rescued the fairy princess.

Although she didn't look much like a fairy, nor did she act like a princess. Considering her mother was a senator and she was a doctor, Bobby had figured he'd have more prima donna behavior out of Jane Harker. He'd been pleasantly surprised.

"Let's go," he said, and bent down so she could climb on his back again. Instead, Lucky licked him on the chin.

"Ack." Bobby straightened so fast his spine crackled. He wiped the slobber from his face and turned toward the doctor just in time to see her give a sharp yank on her T-shirt. It split at the midriff, exposing smooth, creamy skin and six-pack abs. She hadn't gotten those by walking.

"I thought you brought a first aid kit," he said.

"Band-Aids and antibiotic ointment ain't gonna help this," she muttered, dropping to the ground.

After yanking off her shoe, she began to wrap her ankle with the cloth. Bobby frowned at the difficulty she had with the simple task.

"What happened to your wrist?"

"I landed on it when those guys started shooting and we hit the dirt."

Bobby remembered dumping her and going for his gun.

"I'm sorry, Doctor. I didn't—"

"Jane."

He blinked, then stared at her, confused. "What?"

"Isn't it time you started calling me Jane?"

Breaking her wrist should put him in the doghouse and not on a first-name basis.

"Don't apologize," she said. "I'd rather have a banged-up wrist than a bullet in the head."

Bobby wasn't sure what to make of her. Most

women of his acquaintance would be screaming or crying by now, maybe both, even without the sprained ankle and the injured wrist.

The least he could do was help, so Bobby went down on his knee and reached for the strip of T-shirt.

She shoved at him with her shoulder. "I can do it."

"I can do it faster."

Their eyes met. Hers were narrow but curious, and he found himself captivated by the shade, which made him think of jaguars and cougars. Not exactly an appealing thought out here where the wild things roamed.

Bobby set his hands over hers, and then he didn't want to let go. Her skin was soft and firm. Speckled with calluses and cuts, both rough and gentle, strong yet feminine.

An odd current seemed to pass between them and she cleared her throat, then shoved her foot in Bobby's direction. "Do your worst, soldier boy."

I'd like to do you.

The crude thought, coming out of nowhere, disturbed him, and Bobby quickly wrapped her ankle, taking care not to touch any more of her than was necessary. Touching Jane Harker was both the worst, and the best, idea he'd had in a long time.

Just because he hadn't had sex in months didn't mean he should lust after the first female who came near him. He'd gone longer without a woman. Was this some kind of defense mechanism fashioned by his brain to make him forget Marlie?

Bobby grabbed on to that explanation. Of course. He was on the rebound, so he'd become attracted to the next woman who crossed his path. All he had to do was ignore the lust, and it would go away. So why did that seem easier thought than done?

He finished wrapping her ankle and Jane stood, waving away his aid with an annoyed look. Taking help from others was obviously not something she did with any grace. Just like Bobby himself.

Tentatively she put weight on her ankle. He watched her face, but she didn't wince. She didn't comment, either.

"Well?" he pressed.

"Just a twinge. I'll be fine."

"I don't want you ruining anything. I can carry you."

"I'm sure you can. However, I choose not to be carried."

"But—"

"Choice, Luchetti. It's the American way."

"We're in Mexico."

She glared at him before walking across the tiny clearing, then back without a limp. Her ankle seemed all right, and he had to admit, though never to her or anyone else, she *was* kind of heavy.

"We've lost a lot of daylight," he said. "We need to move fast if we want to reach the airfield before dark."

"I'll manage, Captain."

"Great." He leaned over, snatching his weapons and her backpack off the ground. "And the name's Bobby."

He set off down the trail. The maniacs who'd shot at them might have headed toward the village, but there were no rules that said they couldn't return— with reinforcements of both men and ammunition.

He glanced at Dr. Harker. Why did they want her so bad?

JANE CAUGHT BOBBY Luchetti staring at her midriff more than once. What was wrong with the man? Her belly wasn't anything to write home about. She'd lifted and carried so many supplies, children and elderly that her stomach muscles were as hard as a board. She'd never possess the soft and feminine curves of a supermodel.

Jane gave a mental snort. *As if.*

Perhaps he was just wondering how she could have the guts to expose her…gut. But Jane didn't put much stock in appearances. Why bother when her appearance would never be fashionable?

She was strong, smart and good at what she did, which was enough. It had to be.

"How much longer?" she asked.

"Soon."

Jane had to wonder if his idea of *soon* and hers had anything in common.

Lucky trotted between them, tongue lolling. The dog liked taking a walk, even when it was a hundred and ten degrees in the shade.

Jane wiped another wash of sweat from her brow. More like a hundred and twenty. She pulled a bottle of water from her bag and drank half.

Nothing like warm water on a hot day. *Blech.* She gave the rest to the dog.

A curse made her look up. Bobby crouched behind a low range of bushes. Jane didn't have to ask what was the matter. Once she joined him, she saw for herself.

The airfield was deserted—except for the mangled plane and several bodies.

"Who the hell is after you?" Luchetti muttered. "What did you do? What do you know?"

Jane kept her mouth shut. Even if she had the answers to those questions she wouldn't have been able to speak. Her tongue felt glued to her teeth. She'd been scared in her hut last night, shaken by the gunfight today. But those bodies, that plane, the spooky, abandoned air of the place made her want to crawl back into the jungle and hide.

Lucky whimpered, and Jane put her hand on the dog's bony head. "What happened?" she whispered.

"They got here before us. But I can't see how. Or why."

His eyes narrowed on the airfield, then he gave the trees and the foliage a good stare, too.

"Who're they?"

"No clue. I'd like to get my hands on the radio in that hut, but I have a feeling that's what they're after."

"Meaning?"

"Booby trap. Or maybe just a trap." He went silent and thoughtful for several moments before lifting his head. "We're going to have to move on."

"Where?"

"Nearest large city is...Puerto?" She nodded. "There'll be a phone. I can make a call and get you out of here."

Jane contemplated the bodies. Someone wanted her dead very badly. She wasn't sure if walking through the jungle was the best idea. Then again, she didn't have a better one.

"You okay?"

His rough fingers brushed her elbow. The texture should have been unpleasant, even startling, but the slight contact, the heat, the strength of him soothed her.

Jane took a deep breath. "This has never happened to me before."

"What?"

"Bullets flying, people dying, strangers trying to kill me."

Bobby's hand dropped back to his side. "Happens to me all the time."

CHAPTER FOUR

BOBBY COULDN'T COUNT the number of occasions he'd been forced to flee through enemy territory. He much preferred chasing to being pursued—who wouldn't?—but his preferences were rarely consulted when the army made a game plan.

Usually he was dressed like a local and could blend right in. However, since he'd been told this mission was a simple in and out, he hadn't taken the time to create a disguise. Therefore, he appeared to be exactly what he was—an American Special Forces operative sporting bright blue eyes in a country full of brown ones. He suddenly missed his contacts as much as he missed his mommy.

Even if he'd been able to blend in, the doctor and her ugly dog would stand out like processed white bread at a health food store.

Well, maybe not the dog. Bobby glanced at the one-eyed, mangy mutt that sat next to Dr. Harker's foot preening as if she were the most recent elect to Best in Show. There were a thousand dogs just like Lucky all over Mexico—except they were better-looking.

Bobby lifted his gaze. Pale skin, light eyes and

hair, Jane didn't fit in, either. One look and anyone would know she was an Ivy League physician playing at poverty. He didn't want to imagine what would happen if the men who were after them got their hands on her. Unfortunately, he kept imagining it.

"We need to move," he snapped. "Step where I step. Don't wander off."

He expected a sarcastic comment, but Jane merely nodded and inched closer. He caught the scent of a storm on the air and glanced at the sky.

"What?" She followed his gaze.

"I smell a storm, but…there's not a cloud anywhere."

He sniffed again. That scent was coming from her hair.

"Oh!" Jane's hand went to her head. "I rinsed with rainwater."

Bobby gritted his teeth. How was a man supposed to *think* when a woman smelled like that?

He shook his head, trying to clear the cobwebs and the lust. He had better luck with the cobwebs. As soon as he got out of this jungle he was going to get laid—twice.

"Why should I step where you step?" she asked.

He thought of the demolition someone had stolen from him. "Could be trip wires."

"Trip wires?" Her face paled. "Like in Vietnam?"

"Like in every sweaty country. Don't worry. I doubt they had time to wire the whole jungle, even if they do know how."

When she didn't laugh, Bobby sighed. "I'm just

being cautious. I've seen a hundred places just like this."

"A hundred?"

He shrugged. "I've had sand duty lately, but I know what to look for. Relax."

She stared into his eyes for several seconds, then nodded. "I'm sure my mother would only send the best."

"Your mother didn't send me. Only the army can do that."

"You obviously don't know my mother." She smiled. "Forget it, Luchetti. I promise I won't wander off. How long until we reach Puerto?"

"Several hours. If we're lucky."

She glanced at the sky. "It'll be dark before then."

"I know. We'll have to hole up somewhere."

She nodded again, accepting the inevitable.

"Who do you think did this?" Jane waved at the decimated airfield. "Couldn't have been the guys who were shooting at us."

Bobby cocked his head. Clever girl.

"You killed most of them, didn't you?"

Which had seemed to bother her a lot when it happened. Funny what a few more dead bodies did for the attitude. Or maybe not so funny.

"Most," he agreed. But not all.

The ones who were left had scampered off in the direction of the village. Not that they couldn't have doubled back. However, Bobby didn't think two men, no matter how well supplied, could have caused this amount of destruction.

If they had, where were they? They should have hidden, then snatched Jane—at the very least killed both her and Bobby. It's what he would have done.

Which led him to the same conclusion the doctor had made. There were two gangs with guns in the jungle. And wasn't that just special?

Bobby started off through the dense brush, using his knife to clear a better path whenever necessary.

"I don't understand what's going on here," she muttered.

Lucky muttered, too, but the dog stopped her odd canine "talking" at a glare from Bobby.

"How many people are trying to kill me? And why?"

"If you figure it out, clue me in. Now, let's make some time."

The doctor kept pace with him, and she didn't complain. She didn't limp, either.

"Ankle better?"

"Hard to say. I wrapped it tight enough to walk. When I take off the binding, it'll probably swell like a blowfish. So I guess I won't take off the binding."

"Your wrist?"

"Bruised."

He glanced back as she held up her hand. A dark blotch had already materialized against the pale skin of her wrist. Bobby winced. "Sorry."

"Once again, Captain, better a bruise and a sprain than a funeral. Have I thanked you for saving my life?"

"Just part of the service included with your taxes, ma'am."

"Nevertheless, I apologize for nearly gutting you and for arguing."

"You couldn't have gutted me, and the arguments were...refreshing."

"I suppose people kowtow to you all the time?"

"Unless they're terrorists or psychotics. *They* don't usually spare the time for chatter before they try to kill me."

"Nice life you lead."

"I wouldn't be throwing stones in a glass jungle, if I were you."

"How do you stand it?" she whispered.

"It isn't so bad."

People trying to kill him were a fact of Bobby's life. Maybe he'd gotten a bit tired of it lately, but that didn't mean he wasn't going back for more.

He believed in what he did, knew that without his expertise in fighting for truth, justice and the American Way, shit would happen.

As Colin was fond of saying: shit was inevitable.

For an instant, Bobby missed his brother so badly his stomach ached. Until he'd turned eighteen and enlisted, Bobby and Colin had been roommates.

Back home, there'd been three bedrooms for six children. Kim, by virtue of being the only girl, received her own room. No one complained. She'd been snarky from birth.

Another had gone to Evan, Dean and Aaron. Evan was laid-back, Dean terminally pissed off, and Aaron...Aaron was a saint in Luchetti clothing.

Or he had been until he'd turned his back on the

priesthood. No one had known why until a few years ago when his fourteen-year-old daughter by a Las Vegas stripper had show up on the doorstep. *Oops.*

Which left the last room for Bobby and Colin—two boys who couldn't have been more different. Colin loved books, words, pictures of far-off places. He'd studied constantly to get a scholarship to Boston University.

Bobby had played every sport in high school, excelling at football and wrestling. For some reason he'd been gifted with a good portion of the Luchetti family brains. All he had to do was look at his notes and an A on the test was his.

He'd used the time everyone else spent studying to work out, honing his body so he'd be ready to join the army at eighteen. While Colin dreamed of writing about exotic lands, Bobby dreamed of saving the world.

They'd fought over everything—in Luchetti land fighting was considered a pastime, not a crime—but they'd never fought over a woman. None of them had.

The Luchetti brothers had a code—unwritten, but also unbreakable, or at least it had been.

Never touch your brother's girl.

Bobby shoved the memories from his mind, but the ache in his belly remained. Would he ever get rid of it?

BOBBY HAD GONE SILENT. Jane could practically see the intense thoughts rolling off him like steam in a jungle dawn. She hoped he was formulating a plan to get them out of here, preferably without body bags.

She kept quiet and walked in his footsteps. Lucky slunk behind Jane, glancing far too often into the steadily darkening brush. The dog wasn't any more happy about being out here at night than Jane was.

Bobby stopped so abruptly Jane nearly ran into his broad back. Nervous, she peeked around his shoulder, expecting at any moment to get her head blown off by a renegade member of a drug cartel, or the men who wanted to kill her. Which would it be? What did it matter? A gun was a gun and dead was dead.

"We'll stop here," Bobby said.

She glanced around the overgrown path that passed for a trail. "Right here?"

"*Right* here wouldn't be all that bright, now would it?"

"Not like this is Route 66."

Bobby lifted, then lowered, one shoulder. Jane touched her mouth to make sure the drool hadn't escaped. She must have contracted a tropical fever to suddenly become light-headed over the rippling muscles of soldier boy. Hopefully the disease wasn't fatal.

"There's water over there." He waved vaguely to the right.

"And you know this how?"

"Can't you smell it?"

Jane sniffed. All she could smell was him.

While that should be unpleasant after a day in the

sun and the heat, she had to admit the scent made her light-headed again.

Definitely jungle fever.

He pushed through the dense brush lining the trail, and Jane scrambled to keep up. Lucky raced off as if she'd just seen a rabbit, and Jane took a quick step after her.

Bobby put out his arm. "Listen."

Splash.

He'd been right about the water.

Hoping for paradise—a gilded cove with glistening turquoise water—Jane eagerly followed Bobby through the greenery. She'd just begun a lovely fantasy where the two of them frolicked naked beneath a waterfall, and no one wanted to kill her, when he stopped again. This time she did run into him. Jane nearly fell on her butt before she gained her balance by catching Bobby's shoulders.

"Damn," he muttered.

Jane jerked her hands away as if he were a hot potato. Nevertheless, she could still feel the heat of his skin and the solid weight of his muscles against her palms. Peeking around his shoulder for a second time, Jane repeated the curse.

Lucky lolled in the center of a very large mud puddle.

"Get her out of there before she grinds all of our drinking water into her mangy hide."

"Lucky, no!" Jane called.

The dog turned her single eye in Jane's direction and snorted, then she flipped onto her back and wiggled.

"Isn't she too refined for mud wrestling?"

"That's called a mud bath," Jane murmured. "They're good for the complexion."

Not to mention cool on heated mangy hides.

Luchetti shot Jane an incredulous look, as if waiting for her to laugh. But she wasn't joking.

"There has to be more water than this," he muttered, and stalked past the dog.

There *were* several more puddles farther into the brush. Thankfully, Lucky was already covered in mud and didn't feel the need to roll in every one of them.

The water had gathered in a basin. Bobby climbed the small incline that led to an escarpment of dirt topped with vegetation and backed by a small cliff. He tossed her backpack to the ground, then laid his rifle next to it.

"Is this safe?" Jane nearly moaned out loud at the pleasure of leaving her feet.

"Safe as we'll get. With my back to the wall, I can see anyone approaching from that direction. Should be able to hear them, too. Fire wouldn't be a good idea, though. Cold camp tonight."

"No problem."

The idea of a fire in this climate was downright nauseating.

Luchetti sat and nudged the backpack in Jane's direction. "So, what's for dinner?"

Jane opened the bag. "Four juice boxes and two packages of crackers."

"Split it up."

"You think we'll be somewhere sane by tomorrow?"

"Doubtful. But we should be somewhere that has food."

Jane divided the provisions. "You don't have much use for Mexico, do you?"

"I don't have much use for a lot of places. Don't take it personally."

"I like it here." She stabbed the straw through the tiny hole in the juice box. "Or at least I did."

"You have any idea why someone wants to kill you?"

"None."

"How about kidnapping?"

"Well, my mother isn't hurting for money."

"Weird," he murmured. "If they're áfter ransom, they should be more careful where their bullets are flying."

"You won't get any argument from me."

"And Enrique definitely wanted to kill you."

Jane stilled at the memory, which upset her more than the drug dealers in the jungle. Enrique had been her friend. Why would he try to kill her?

"Speaking of Enrique," she said. "Is he…?"

"Dead? I hope so."

Jane kind of did, too, and that was so unlike her she had to fight back an annoying urge toward tears. She hadn't cried yet, and she wasn't going to start now.

"There must be two groups after you," Bobby murmured. "But why?"

Excellent question. Jane had always wondered what it would feel like to be popular. She didn't like it.

Jane watched as Bobby fumbled the small juice box with his big hands. "Let me."

The punch of his blue eyes was like a fist to her solar plexus. Men shouldn't have eyes that pretty.

"I can—" Sighing, he shoved the mangled straw and box into her hands. "I can't. Why do they make those things so small?"

Even though his gesture was impatient, Jane shivered at the scrape of his skin against hers and botched her first attempt.

"They're for children." She pushed her thumbnail into the hole and inserted the straw easily on her second try. "Not Captain America."

He gave a short, surprised bark of laughter.

"What?" she asked.

"My brothers always called me G.I. Joe. Still do."

Jane handed Bobby the box and some of the crackers. "Your family doesn't approve of your career?"

"They don't like it when I disappear. Sometimes months, even a year can go by without a word from me. Can't say I blame them."

"What about your wife?"

He stiffened. "Not married."

From his reaction, Jane figured there was more to that story, but she didn't know him well enough to pry. At least she could put aside the nagging guilt over the lust she couldn't seem to control.

He wasn't married. Hallelujah.

Lucky dropped next to Jane, smudging mud all over her right thigh. After the day she'd had, the extra dirt was hardly noticeable. What Jane wouldn't give for a hot shower and a glass of red wine. Not that she'd seen either one since coming to Mexico more than a year ago.

Jane split her crackers with the dog. Instead of wolfing them down like a dog should, Lucky nibbled daintily on them one at a time.

"You shouldn't give her half," Bobby protested. "Dogs can go a long time without eating."

"I couldn't enjoy my share if Lucky went hungry."

"I've never understood people who treat their pets like children."

"I'd never treat Lucky like a child. She wouldn't allow it. She's my friend." Jane patted the bony head. "Don't you have a pet?"

"I don't even have an address."

"Stupid question. I meant *haven't* you ever had a pet?"

"Not really. Farm dogs are working animals. The cats come and go—and they multiply like rabbits. They're hunters and not exactly cuddly. Not that I'd cuddle with them or anything."

He made a manly face and flexed his muscles.

Jane laughed, even though she wanted to throw herself into his lap and touch all of his bronzed, rippling skin. The jungle brain-rot fever was back.

"It's strange how reality and belief can be so different," she murmured.

At his questioning glance, she continued. "I lived in big cities and apartment buildings most of my life. I figured all the farm kids had pets up the wazoo, and I envied them. I couldn't have a pet because Mother was allergic to cats."

"What about a dog?"

"Dogs and apartments don't go together very well."

Or at least that had been her mother's excuse. When Jane was sent off to boarding school, the whole issue became moot.

Her childhood desire for a pet explained why she'd fallen in love with Lucky at first sight. Or maybe it was just her lack of friends and the compulsive desire to help anyone or anything she considered helpless.

"Never occurred to me that on the farm, animals are for work."

"Or food," he added.

She winced.

"You aren't a vegetarian, are you?"

He said the word as some people might say *republican*—or *democrat*.

"No, but I prefer not to meet my food, not to acknowledge it might once have been furry and cute. I like my sustenance packaged in plastic with a lovely price sticker on the front."

He shook his head. "Then why are you here?"

"Because I can make a difference."

He stared at her for a long, charged moment, then nodded. "Me, too."

BOBBY WATCHED REALIZATION spread across Dr. Harker's face. They both wanted to save the world—just in different ways.

He also saw the exact moment she rejected his way and stiffened. "Killing people can make a difference?"

"If they're the right people."

She made a disgusted sound deep in her throat and began to rummage in her backpack again.

"I do more than kill."

She glanced at him. "Like what?"

Lie. Cheat. Steal. Infiltrate. Search. Destroy.

He doubted Jane would approve of his usual activities.

"Anything else in there?" Bobby flicked a finger at the backpack.

She stared at him for another second, green-brown eyes glinting in the fading, tropical light. Night approached. Soon they'd have nothing but each other—and the dog.

"Animal cookies," Jane announced.

"Is that some euphemism for bullsh—"

"Hey!" She shook two yellow cartons with caged giraffes, zebras and elephants imprinted on their sides. "They're *actually* animal cookies. Gutter brain."

Bobby smiled. Dr. Harker was a lot like his sister, and he liked his sister. Hell, he liked Jane. Which was damned odd.

She was everything that usually annoyed him. A do-gooder who got herself into impossible situations. A bleeding heart who sneered at military necessity. Of course they were always the first ones whining for help in a crisis. Just look at her mother.

Jane tossed one of the cardboard boxes into his lap. He stared at the bright colors. "My niece loves these," he murmured.

"You're close?"

"Never met her."

"Does she live in Botswana?"

"Then I'd have seen her. She lives in Illinois, near my parents."

"When was the last time you were home?"

"Not sure. Before my niece Zsa-Zsa arrived, anyway. Probably longer."

He'd been offered leaves. He'd taken another mission instead.

"I'll go home as soon as you're safe," Bobby said.

"Promise?"

He lifted his gaze to hers. "You'll be safe. I promise."

She rolled her eyes. "Not that. Promise you'll go home."

"I guess."

"What's so bad about home?"

"Nothing."

Right before he'd met her he'd even been pining for the place.

"It's just—"

How could he explain that the farm that meant so much to his parents, his brother, meant nothing to him? Every time he went there he couldn't wait to leave. He didn't like planting; he couldn't stand cows. He loved his family but—

"The farm isn't for you," she finished.

"Yeah."

"My mother's life isn't for me. Meetings, parties, power. She doesn't understand how I can prefer a hut to a penthouse."

"I have to agree with her there."

"You'd like to live in a penthouse?"

"Only if it was a good way to infiltrate a terrorist organization."

She shook her head. "Why do you see a terrorist around every corner?"

"Because there is."

"Paranoid," she muttered.

"Not in my world."

In his world there *was* a terrorist on every corner. Or at least behind every seemingly innocent face.

He'd seen children blow up checkpoints in a land that was supposed to be promised. Locked up women who smuggled weapons and firearms beneath their dresses, pretending to be pregnant when they were merely insane. He'd met men who held out one hand in friendship, while hiding a grenade in the other.

"I don't like your world," she said.

"I'm not wild about it myself."

"Why don't you quit?"

His mother asked the same thing every time he spoke with her, and he gave Jane the same answer.

"If I don't try to save the world, who will?"

CHAPTER FIVE

JANE LAY WITH HER HEAD pillowed on her backpack, staring at the stars. He wanted to save the world.

She found that more attractive than deep blue eyes and great, big biceps.

His was a foolish wish but an admirable one. A goal Jane could get behind since she had the same delusion herself. Interesting that their wants were the same, yet their methods were completely different. Of course there was a whole lot of world to be saved.

Staring at the sky brought that truth home. Under the vastness of a midnight universe, her life seemed very small.

The men who were trying to kill her must have the same thought. She shivered, even though the night was warm.

Lucky pressed against her leg, heated body covered with scratchy dried mud, both comfort and discomfort in one package. Jane put her hand on the dog's head and shifted so she could see Bobby.

He sat with his back against the dirt face of the cliff, rifle across his knees. He'd said he would keep watch until sunrise. She had no doubt that he would.

"I don't think I've ever stayed awake all night," she murmured.

His eyes, which had been scanning the trees, the valley, the sky, flicked to hers. "What about a giggling-girl party?"

"Never heard of it."

"Where did you live, under a rock?"

"Boarding school. Close enough."

"I'd think you would have been up giggling every night in that case."

"You've never been to an all-girl boarding school, have you?"

"No." He gave an exaggerated sigh of disappointment, which made her laugh.

"I was too tall and too…robust to be popular. Too much of an egghead to be witty."

"That doesn't sound like much fun."

Jane didn't want to remember her past; she wanted to hear about his. What kind of a family produced soldier boys?

"You have a brother and a sister?"

"I have four brothers and a sister." At her incredulous expression, he continued. "Farm family— need a lotta hands. We were all born a year or so a part."

"And your mother's not psychotic?"

"Depends on which day you talk to her."

Jane tilted her head, but he was grinning. "Mom was tough. Couldn't get much past that woman. Considering we grew up without turning into serial killers or bums, she did all right."

"What *did* you become?"

"My oldest brother was almost a priest."

Jane had never known anyone who'd almost been a priest. Technically, she still didn't.

"Aaron's a…well, professional do-gooder, for want of a better term. He and his wife run a home for runaways in Las Vegas."

Sounded like something the senator would be interested in funding. If she could get enough publicity out of it.

"My sister, Kim, is studying to be a lawyer, which is pretty amazing since she has a two-year-old. Her husband's a farmer, same as my brother, Dean."

"Is Dean the one who's left-handed?"

"Yeah. He took over the farm from my father a few years back, though not without a struggle. Dad wasn't ready to give it up. Until he had a heart attack. He and my mom live in the big house, and Dean shares the thresher's cottage with his son."

"And Dean's wife?"

"No wife. Just Tim."

"How did he manage that?"

"Tim was abandoned in Las Vegas. My niece brought him home."

"Like a puppy?"

"She does that. So did her dad."

"Pretty precocious for a two-year-old."

"Not Zsa-Zsa. Rayne."

Jane's head spun with all the names. "How many nieces do you have?"

"Zsa-Zsa—her real name is Glory—is Kim's

daughter. Rayne is Aaron's and she's fourteen, and then there's Aaron's latest, Faith. She's…new."

"You don't know how old?"

"I was out of the country at the time. I'm just glad I remembered her name."

"What about nephews?"

"One." He frowned. "Two."

"The family's expanding so rapidly you can't keep track?"

"Pretty much. My youngest brother, Evan, just got married. He and his wife own a bed-and-breakfast in Arkansas."

Jane counted on her fingers. One. Two. Three. Four. Five. "You're missing one."

"What?"

"One brother. Aaron. Dean. Evan. That leaves you and…?"

"Colin."

The way he said the name, then stared at the sky again, disturbed Jane. She could think of a lot of bad things that could have happened to Colin. The curse of being a doctor.

"Is he all right?" she asked, when Bobby continued to stare at the sky and scowl.

"Better off than me," Bobby muttered. "Get some sleep, Jane. Tomorrow could be rougher than today."

She opened her mouth to ask more, then thought better of it. Bobby had answered every question, except the last, with nothing but honesty. His reluctance to discuss one brother should be respected.

So why did it only make her more curious?

NIGHTS TOOK FOREVER to pass when you were all alone and wide awake. Thankfully Jane had drifted off after only forty-five minutes of shifting, mumbling and cursing. Sleeping on the hard ground wasn't for civilians. However, Bobby could sleep anywhere—or not sleep at all as the occasion warranted.

Field sleep had been part of his training for Delta Force. When on a mission with his twelve-man team, someone was always on guard. So Bobby learned to fall asleep quickly before it was his turn to take the watch.

But when he was on a singleton, he slipped into field sleep, where his mind rested but was also alert for the slightest noise or movement. In that case he became instantly and completely aware.

He'd been educated in other tactics, such as slowing his heart rate to fire a sniper rifle between beats. When doing such intricate shooting, the mere thump of the heart could throw a bullet off by several feet at long range.

In cold weather, or icy countries, Bobby possessed the ability to warm a trigger finger, or nearly frostbitten toes, by directing the flow of blood to the extremities through consciousness of mind.

SERE training had taught him how to stay awake for days—one of the first things an enemy did to a captive was to deprive him of sleep—without feeling the strain. This mind-over-matter method also allowed Bobby to watch a building or a subject for long periods without losing his concentration. Delta operators called this the drone zone, where the body became impervious to aches, pains and exhaustion.

Lucky gave a low *woof* and stared at the trees. An instant later an iguana slowly poked its head into the moonlight.

Concerned the dog would chase the reptile and Jane would chase the dog and then they'd have chaos, Bobby said, "Stay," low and stern.

Lucky tilted her head, then laid it over Jane's back, her single eye focused unwaveringly on Bobby.

"Yeah, I wouldn't trust me, either."

If the dog knew his secret thoughts, she'd probably go for Bobby's throat. Ever since Jane had ripped her shirt and bared her belly, he'd been having short, lustful fantasies, which disturbed him a lot. Shouldn't he be thinking about Marlie?

Three months ago he would have taken this alone time to stare at her picture and imagine her face when he knocked on her door at last. However, the thoughts that used to keep him company in the field no longer held any appeal. Thinking of his brother's wife with too much fondness skirted too close to lines he would never cross, even if Colin had.

In truth, he should be glad he was attracted to someone else. Didn't that prove he was moving on?

He sighed. It would if he could stop feeling so guilty about it.

Bobby and the dog kept vigil as the moon crossed the sky. Lucky didn't sleep any more than Bobby did. Every time a reptile skittered too close, or a mosquito buzzed too loudly, Lucky grumbled. Nothing was going to sneak up on them while she was on the job.

Dawn was still a hint on the horizon when Bobby relaxed into field sleep. He hadn't been there for ten minutes when he felt something out of place. Slowly he opened his eyes, scanned the forest. Had he been dreaming?

Not likely. Bobby didn't do much dreaming. Probably a result of his odd sleeping habits.

What would be the point, anyway? He'd only get interrupted when the dreaming got good.

So if something had disturbed him, why hadn't Lucky barked? Bobby shifted his gaze and nearly swallowed his tongue.

Both the dog and the woman were gone.

JANE CAME AWAKE IN the darkest part of the night—after the moon had disappeared and before the sun rose—with an impossible urge to pee. Didn't that just figure?

She glanced at Bobby, who appeared to be sleeping. Although, she could swear she saw a sliver of white—as if his eyes were still half open—and that just creeped her out.

Should she wake him up and ask for a hall pass to the jungle bidet? The idea was mortifying. She hadn't needed permission since she'd left high school.

Jane sat up. Lucky began to prance.

"Gotta go, too? That's convenient."

Bobby didn't move as they headed for the trees. She still had the distinct sensation he was watching her, so when he didn't call out for her to halt, Jane slipped into the foliage with Lucky.

After completing their business, Lucky trotted toward the water and Jane followed. As long as she was here, she might as well wash her face, rinse her teeth. She had a feeling Luchetti wasn't going to allow much time for grooming.

Jane reached the small indentations filled with water to find Lucky already body-deep in mud. "You are *not* going to be welcomed on that airplane."

Or in Washington, for that matter. Good thing Jane didn't plan on staying.

She knelt next to the largest puddle. "I'll just find out when my mother lost her mind and be on my way."

Bobby would be on his way, too. Probably today. The thought made Jane melancholy.

Annoyed that she could become attached to someone so quickly—how pathetic was that?—Jane scooped lukewarm water into her palms and splashed her face. The soft shuffle of a boot made her open her eyes.

"Bobby?" she said, just as Lucky erupted into her drug-dealer snarl.

"JANE!"

Bobby wasn't proud. He'd shout down the forest if she'd only answer.

That she didn't had him very worried. She

couldn't have gone far. Only to the water, or the nearest open-air latrine. Maybe she was embarrassed to answer while she was otherwise engaged.

"Lucky!"

He doubted the dog would have the same problem.

The only reason Jane and Lucky had gotten away was because he'd tuned his ear to the animal's nervous mumbles. When there hadn't been one, he hadn't awoken.

"Stupid!" he muttered. "Trust yourself. Nothing and one else."

Since the dog had better ears and a nastier disposition, Bobby had to conclude that no one had entered their camp and spirited them away. Jane and Lucky had left of their own free will, which meant they had to be around here somewhere.

So why wouldn't they answer?

The ground on their plateau was hard and dry. Not a footstep to be followed. But when he neared the water, he discovered both a foot and a pawprint.

"Jane! Lucky!" His voice sounded angry and scared—which was exactly how he felt.

If she was messing with him—something he'd expect of his brothers but not of a do-gooder physician—he'd, he'd...

Well, he couldn't kick her ass, but he'd think of something.

However, if she *wasn't* messing with him—and the more time that passed the less likely that seemed—they were both in deep trouble.

Terrified he'd find Jane's body, or worse, Bobby

rushed to the watering hole and found more paw-prints, as well as more footprints. A lot bigger ones than Jane's.

Unfortunately, once they reached the jungle, the tracks disappeared. The ground was too dry for an imprint.

So Bobby followed procedure, trekking in steadily larger sweeps, around the water, deeper and deeper into the trees, but he found nothing.

Which was as impossible as it was annoying. He stopped and glanced at a sky filled with pink, orange and red streaks of light.

It was as if Jane and Lucky had been plucked out of the jungle.

Disgusted with himself, Bobby almost missed the only clue he had. A small broken branch and half of a bootprint dug into the softer, wetter ground beneath a fern. He was headed in the right direction.

Since he hadn't found any blood or bodies, who-ever had snatched Jane and Lucky didn't want them dead. Yet. Which was confusing as hell.

Yesterday they hadn't been so picky.

So were these the same guys with different orders? Or different guys? The only thing that really mattered was who was giving those orders.

They'd gotten a decent head start on him. Never-theless, he'd catch up. Eventually.

What he couldn't figure out was why they'd left him alive. Not that they'd have been able to kill him—he hadn't been that out of it. Still, they had to know he'd follow, and that he'd be pissed.

Bobby stopped dead in the middle of the jungle. Was that what they were after? Could the nefarious kidnappers be trying to get their hands on him and not Jane, after all?

Which made no sense; no one should know he was here. Besides, he hadn't done anything secret or underhanded in Mexico.

"Lately," he muttered.

Bobby gave up worrying about the reasons as he tried to make some time. But having to stop and hunt for clues kept slowing him down.

The kidnappers weren't following a path, or at least not one Bobby could see. The jungle was dense, and the ground dry. But he wasn't called G.I. Joe for nothing. He might lose the trail once in a while, but he always found it again.

Dawn gave way to midmorning. Bobby headed into the thick of Quintana Roo. They were traveling away from Puerto. Didn't that just figure?

He came to a small river, what they'd call a creek—pronounced crick—back home. Bobby knelt at the edge and doused his head.

With water trickling over his face, down his neck, he let his gaze wander over the area. A patch of garish yellow stuck out of the shallows on the other side.

Bobby strode across, letting the just-cooler-than-tepid water soothe his feet inside his boots. Bending over, he snatched a stray piece of cardboard from the silt.

To anyone else, it was garbage. To Bobby, a billboard. Jane was alive and kicking.

With a thin smile, he tucked the empty container of animal cookies into his pocket, then stilled. A splash was his only warning before someone knocked him over the head.

Or tried to. The instant he heard the sound, Bobby ducked, twisted, turned. The butt end of a rifle slammed into his shoulder.

He gritted his teeth against the pain, then grabbed the weapon and yanked it out of the hands of what appeared to be a guerrilla fighter.

Bobby popped him in the jaw. His attacker went down, and he didn't get up.

While he was sleeping, Bobby relieved him of all of his toys: AK-47—weapon of distinguished evildoers everywhere—9 mm Beretta and a huge machete. The guy wore camouflage pants, shirt, military boots, he'd even painted his face to match the rest.

"An awful lot of trouble you went to, *amigo*."

When the guy's eyelids fluttered, Bobby pressed the machete tightly against his throat. His eyes shot open.

"Who are you?" Bobby asked.

"No habla."

"You better *habla* quick or you'll be *habla-ing* without an Adam's apple."

He pricked the skin and blood welled. So did the words. Unfortunately, they were all in Spanish.

"Hold on," Bobby barked.

The man knew enough to shut up. Probably more from the knife at his throat and Bobby's tone of voice than anything else.

People north of the Rio Grande believed that everyone south of it spoke a good deal of English, but they didn't. Spanish was their language. Only Americans believed that everyone in every country should be able to converse in English at their command.

Bobby searched his tiny arsenal of español.

"Quienes?"

"Roberto."

They had the same name. How convenient.

"Qué pasa?"

He felt foolish saying "what's happening?" like a sitcom star or a guy in an annoying beer commercial, but his options were few.

The guy started blabbering again. Bobby grasped a few words. *Mujer*. Woman. *Perro*. Dog. That much he knew.

"Por que?" he asked. *Why?*

"Ella debe morir."

That was a toughie. *Ella* meant she. *Debe?* No clue. But *morir,* he kind of thought that meant *die*. But if they wanted Jane dead, why had they kidnapped her?

He didn't know how to ask that. But he could ask where.

"Dónde?"

"Dónde?" The man's beady black eyes shifted left, right, back to Bobby's, then left again. *"No sé."*

"You don't know? Why don't I believe that?" He pressed the knife harder against Roberto's throat. *"Dónde?"*

Roberto spilled everything he knew. Too bad Bobby didn't understand any of it.

He didn't have time to decipher the directions, nor to query why the guy hadn't just shot him—or at least tried to. Bobby tied up Roberto, tossed his guns into the water, then continued to follow Jane's trail.

Despite the time-out for questioning, Bobby caught up to the others by midafternoon when they stopped at a hut very similar to the one where Bobby had found Jane. Several more guerrilla types loitered outside, fingering their weapons and smoking their cigarettes.

He would have thought he'd wandered into a revolution, except those guns were too modern and too expensive for a rebel force. Only illegal narcotics bought such hardware.

Circling the area, Bobby tried to figure out what they were up to. He also wanted to make sure Jane was actually inside before he did anything drastic.

As he inched around the south side of the hut, a familiar snarl froze him in his tracks. He peeked past the structure and found Lucky tied to a tree, kicking up quite a ruckus.

Even without the expensive weaponry, Bobby would have been able to detect drug dealers in the vicinity by the force of Lucky's fury. He only hoped they didn't shoot the dog just to shut her up.

Considering her lack of an eye, Lucky saw pretty

well. Her head swiveled in Bobby's direction and he tensed, afraid she'd give him away. Instead, she stopped snarling and lay down—as if she knew he was here to rescue her; she only had to be patient.

If he'd been in the Middle East, suitably disguised and briefed, Bobby would have walked into that hut and pretended he was one of them. Even without the bright blue eyes, American weapons and army fatigues, he sucked at this language, and he had no idea how many people were inside, let alone what they were up to.

If he went in, guns blazing, people would die, and while that didn't bother him when terrorists or evil drug lords were involved, it did when innocent civilians got caught in the crossfire.

When the innocent civilian was a woman with a sharp mind and an even sharper mouth, soft skin, sweetly scented hair and a body he wanted to spend a week getting to know, Bobby was bothered a lot. Almost as much as he was bothered by his feelings for her in the first place.

So he played it smart. He disabled the guards one at a time, then he peeked into the single window, hoping for a lightning bolt of inspiration that would allow him to extract the doctor with the lowest possible body count.

One look at the scene inside, and he had a hard time remembering why he shouldn't kill them all.

CHAPTER SIX

JANE HAD BEEN BERATING herself for her stupidity from the moment the Little General's men had carted her away.

One of his minions had grabbed Lucky mid-snarl and wrapped her snout with tape. Not that Lucky hadn't continued to snarl, anyway. Jane had been terrified they'd kill the dog to keep her quiet, but they hadn't. Jane had a very bad feeling they were saving that for a later bout of persuasion.

She'd dubbed her captor the Little General because he reminded her of Napoléon. Dark skin, hair, eyes and disposition—no doubt his height was an issue there. She had no idea who he was, but he knew her.

However, he didn't know Bobby, and that fact seemed to have made him slightly unbalanced.

"Who is the American soldier?" he demanded. "Why is he here?"

Jane stared straight ahead and didn't answer.

He backhanded her, and she tasted blood where her teeth had frayed the inside of her lip the last time he'd hit her. Wasn't there some rule about name, rank and serial number?

Or was that only for actual soldiers? Regardless, she wasn't going to tell them about Bobby unless she had to. So far, they hadn't done anything that had made talking inevitable.

"Why would an American soldier rescue a foolish Yankee doctor?" the General demanded. "This makes no sense."

Lucky suddenly stopped snarling. That couldn't be good.

Jane's gaze slid toward the window, and the General pounced. "You think he will come for you? That will be a bit difficult, since I sent Roberto to slit his throat."

Jane made her first sound. She laughed. Right in the General's face.

His eyes widened. His face reddened. He backhanded her twice this time. Left cheek, right cheek—he was ambidextrous. She was going to look like she'd gone ten rounds with the champ.

Jane had lived in rough places for the past few years, but she'd always been protected, cherished, respected. No one had ever touched her with violence—until today. She wasn't sure how long she'd last before she cried.

"The idiots should have gotten rid of him when they came for you, but they were afraid." His lip curled in disgust before he turned on her again. "Why are you being so stubborn, Doctor?"

The General spoke impeccable English. He must have gone to school in the States. But despite his cultured voice, Jane saw the animal lurking in his eyes.

Showing a man like this her fear would be like showing fresh blood to a wolf.

"What is he to you? Mercenary bodyguard? Protection bought by the disillusioned Doctors of Mercy?"

As if the Doctors of Mercy could afford a mercenary. Which was why she'd been gifted with Enrique, who'd obviously been more mercenary than she knew.

Jane continued to stare straight ahead. The General leaned down to study her face—not much of a stretch.

"Lover?" he murmured, and she was so shocked she actually glanced at him. He smirked. "Interesting. You will join him soon. So be not afraid."

Jane rolled her eyes.

"You do not think you will die? That was not the original plan, I must admit. But the orders have changed. Since Enrique botched the job, I must complete it. We have already been paid. However, it disturbed me greatly when one of my men brought the expensive military items he uncovered in the jungle."

Which explained where Bobby's stuff had gone, though not how it had been found. Perhaps an accident, after all.

Jane wanted so badly to ask who had paid the General and why that her lips parted. The man beamed, thinking, no doubt, she would spill her guts in exchange for one more minute of life. He didn't know her very well.

A gunshot sounded. Jane flinched, anticipating

the pain of a bullet, afraid one of the minions had lost patience. He'd no doubt die for disobeying orders, but she'd already be there ahead of him and in no condition to gloat.

Her mouth fell open farther when the toady nearest the door dropped. The one at the window followed before he could even raise his gun.

The cavalry had arrived.

The General called her a vile name in Spanish—one most kids picked up on the street. You'd think a native speaker would have more imagination. He pointed his gun at the dark figure coming through the door, but he couldn't manage to squeeze off a shot before Bobby did.

The man slammed into the floor at Jane's feet, and he didn't move. Nevertheless, Bobby disarmed him and the others before untying Jane.

"Lucky?" she asked, terrified of the answer but needing to know.

"Alive and busy grumbling about the tree she's tied to outside."

Jane let out the breath she'd been holding, then drew it in again as sharp needles of pain shot through her hands when they were released from bondage.

She started to rub them together, but Bobby yanked her into his arms. Shocked, she could only sit there woodenly as he hugged her. He was shaking, but there was nothing sexual about it. He seemed scared, and that made no sense at all. She hadn't thought Bobby Luchetti would be scared of anything.

"You okay?" she asked.

He didn't answer at first. Jane could have sworn he took a whiff of her hair before passing his palm over her head, then releasing her.

"I'm so sorry," he murmured.

Jane glanced at the General. "Yeah, you probably shouldn't have shot *him*."

Bobby's eyes narrowed. He reached out with the tip of one finger and touched her right cheek, her left and finally her mouth. Jane began to tremble.

"He hurt you," he said, as if that explained everything. Maybe it did.

They stared at each other for several charged seconds. Something had changed between them, but Jane wasn't sure what. Then Lucky gave a short, impatient *woof* and the spell was broken.

Bobby began to go through the General's pockets. "Got any idea who this bozo was?"

"None."

He jerked his thumb at the bodies. "How about the bozettes?"

Jane shook her head.

"No ID. Big shock." He searched the others and came up just as empty. Sitting back on his heels, Bobby frowned. "What did he want to know?"

"Who you were. Why you were here. Some of his flunkies found your stuff near the village. That seemed to flip him out."

Bobby's shoulders slumped, and he rubbed his hand over his face before lifting his gaze to hers again. "Why didn't you tell him?"

"He didn't say please."

Bobby's eyebrows rose.

"Besides, once he found out, he'd have killed me and Lucky. I was trying to avoid that."

"You couldn't have avoided it forever."

"I only needed to stay alive until you got here."

"How did you know I'd get here?"

"You're soldier boy. Isn't that your job?"

Bobby heaved himself to his feet, shaking his head, then peered out the hole in the wall. "It was my job to rescue you from a kidnapping by drug dealers."

"You just did."

"Then see you out of this country safely."

"I'm not dead yet."

"I messed up."

"I'm the one who walked into the jungle, alone in the dark. That was stupid."

"I should have—"

"Shoulda, coulda, woulda. Let's just get out of here."

He turned with a puzzled expression. "Weren't you scared?"

"Hell, yes."

"You didn't seem to be."

"Wouldn't have helped. Would probably have hurt. Jerks like these enjoy frightening women. I enjoy screwing up their enjoyment." Jane nudged the General with her foot. "I enjoyed it even more when you screwed up the rest of his life."

"I thought you were a pacifist. That you had no use for guns and soldiers."

"I thought so, too. But I have to admit, Luchetti, I'm glad you were here."

SHE WAS GLAD HE WAS THERE. How was that for a change of heart?

Too bad Bobby still felt like a loser.

"Why shouldn't I have shot this guy?"

He dipped his chin to indicate the man who'd dared to hit Jane. Bobby considered shooting the guy again, but decided that would make him appear a little too gung-ho.

"He said he'd have to finish the job of killing me since Enrique botched it. They'd been paid already."

Jane walked out of the hut and Bobby followed. She made a beeline for Lucky, who began a hyper dance of joy as soon as she saw her mistress.

"Paid?" Bobby asked. "By whom?"

"No clue." Jane released Lucky, then allowed the dog to bathe her face with love. "Which is why you shouldn't have shot him. At least not until he blabbed a name."

"You think he would have?"

"Guys like that always want to tell their victims everything, just before they kill them."

"In the movies, maybe. In real life, not so much."

"Really?"

Bobby nodded.

"I guess you'd know." Jane glanced around the clearing. "He did say their original orders weren't to kill me. I wonder why they changed."

"Guess we'll never know that, either."

Thanks to his happy trigger finger.

"Should we bury them?" Jane asked.

"They wouldn't have buried us."

"That doesn't make it right."

"We don't have time. When these bad guys don't show up at bad-guy headquarters, other bad guys will come searching for them."

Jane frowned. "You don't think this was bad-guy headquarters?"

"Let's find out."

Bobby headed for the stream, planning to re-question the guy he'd tied to a tree, since Jane's Spanish was much better than his. Unfortunately someone had gotten there before them.

He stopped, and Jane ran into his back. He tried to keep her from seeing the body, but it was too late. She made a soft cry of distress at the sight of the man with the machete in his chest.

Bobby urged her into the trees. "We need to get out of here."

"You think they'll come after us because of him?" Jane glanced over her shoulder.

"What are you talking about?"

"I'm sure you had to. But won't that make the others mad?"

"You think *I* killed him?"

Her eyes met his. "Didn't you?"

Bobby searched her face—she didn't seem disgusted or scared—merely curious. The woman continued to amaze him.

"I tied him—alive—to the tree. I couldn't have

him warning his pals that I was on the way. But there wasn't any reason to kill him."

"Then who did?"

"Some guys we really want to avoid," Bobby muttered. "We need to get to Puerto. Preferably yesterday."

"How far?" Jane asked.

"I'm not sure. They dragged you in the other direction."

Jane's shoulders drooped, even as she nodded in acceptance.

Her face was pale, which only made the bruises and the blood stand out even more starkly than before. Bobby wanted to kill those guys all over again.

He withdrew a bandanna from his pocket. "Stay here," he murmured, then glanced at Lucky. "Watch her, girl."

The dog sat down and stared at Jane as if she were the last steak at a barbecue.

"Where…?"

Bobby held up a hand. "Two minutes."

He slipped back to the creek, did a quick perusal of the ground around the dead man. Bootprints. How helpful.

He could probably take the machete along, get it dusted for prints. But what were the odds that the guy who'd killed an assassin in Quintana Roo would have his prints on file with the FBI or even Interpol? Not high enough to warrant touching the gory souvenir and carrying it to the States.

Besides, the killing might not even have anything

to do with them. People were murdered all the time down here.

Bobby left the man and the machete right where they were, then doused his bandanna with cool creek water. Jane was standing exactly where he'd left her. As soon as he stepped out of the trees, Lucky trotted up to him and put her face against his knee.

"I think she loves you."

Horrified, Bobby stared at Lucky, who looked up at him with pure devotion. "What did I do?"

"Saved her life. Just like you saved mine."

Bobby lifted his gaze to Jane's. Sadly her eyes did not carry the same slavish devotion. He offered the dripping bandanna. She stared at it confused.

"For your face. The creek water is cool." He shrugged. "Best I can do right now."

She smiled, then immediately winced as the expression pulled the cut in her lip. But she took the cloth and wiped her face, then pressed it to the worst of the bruises. Ice would help. Unfortunately, they were fresh out. Bobby sighed and headed deeper into the jungle.

"Do I look that bad?" Jane hurried to catch up.

"No," he lied. "Hardly a scratch."

Even Lucky snorted at that.

He set a pace as fast as he thought Jane could manage. They ran across no more cool creeks. There wasn't a renegade block of ice to be had. Neither one of them possessed an aspirin. Jane's Band-Aids would be worthless on two black eyes and a fat lip.

Bobby kept an ear cocked to any sounds on the

trail. Lucky practically walked backward in an attempt to make sure no one else snuck up on them. Amazingly, no one did.

The lack of pursuit made Bobby even more squirrelly than the knowledge of it had. There were at least two bad guys left alive out there, probably more. So why weren't they following with guns blazing?

They reached Puerto without further incident, long after the sun slid below the horizon. The town was large enough to possess a decent hotel with a restaurant, but not too large that there were streetlights on every corner. They were able to slink in the shadows, keeping Jane's battered face and bloody, stained clothes out of sight.

Near the Hotel Puerto, Bobby removed his sidearm and handed it, along with the backpack and rifle, to Jane.

"I doubt they'll rent me a room if I show up armed, with a beat-up woman and a one-eyed dog. Will you be okay for a minute?"

"I'm in a good-size town, with a good-size gun. What could happen?"

Bobby tightened his lips. "I hate it when people say that."

He was able to get two adjacent rooms on the far side of the hotel, away from the lobby. That way they wouldn't have to hoist Lucky by pulley to a second-floor balcony.

"They were okay about the dog?" Jane asked as he handed her a key.

"What they don't know won't hurt them."

"You didn't tell?"

"They didn't ask."

"But—"

"Does Lucky plan on chewing the bedspread? Peeing on the carpet? Clawing the wall?"

Jane stiffened. "Of course not."

"Then she's better behaved than most of the guests. There isn't another hotel, Jane. And you need to eat and sleep. So do I."

She nodded. He could tell she didn't like bending the truth, but she understood the necessity.

They climbed to the second level—always the best choice for security—and Jane opened her door.

"Wait." Bobby stepped in first.

The room was small, a bit shabby, but clean. Though it was unlikely anyone would know they were here, Bobby checked the closet, the bath, under the bed just to be sure.

Lucky trotted in, sniffed one of the double beds, then the other, before choosing the first. Jane tossed her backpack onto the dresser. Leaning over, she stared into the mirror and gently touched the swelling around each eye. "You lied to me."

Bobby, who'd been drifting around the room in search of an ice bucket, paused. "I did?"

"You said I didn't look that bad."

"You don't."

"I suppose you've seen much worse."

She didn't know the half of it. He shrugged and left it at that. "I'm going to get some ice."

"Thanks."

"Then I'll order room service."

She gingerly examined her swollen lower lip. "Probably not a good idea for me to be seen like this in the dining room."

"We shouldn't be seen anywhere. I'm going to call my superior and have a plane here at first light."

"Okay."

Bobby pocketed her key and hurried to the ice machine, concerned at how compliant Jane had become. Though her arguments had been annoying, even life threatening at times, he missed them. And wasn't that just the most foolish thought of all?

He returned, knocking before opening the door an inch.

"Come in."

Jane sat on the bed next to Lucky; both were nearly asleep.

"I don't know if I'll be able to keep my eyes open through dinner."

"Take a shower," Bobby said. "That should help you stay awake. You need to eat, Jane."

She glanced down at herself. "If you haven't noticed, missing a few meals won't hurt me."

He scowled. "I'm not returning you to your mother half sick and beaten to hell."

"My mother's the one who told me I could lose a few pounds."

"Then your mother's the one who should have her head examined first."

She was arguing with him again. Bobby felt so much better.

"Shower." He jabbed a finger at the bathroom. "Ice. Food. Sleep."

She flipped him a salute. "Your wish is my command, Captain."

JANE FLICKED THE SECURITY lock on her door, then punched the button on the bathroom doorknob as well. Foolish, since the guys who were after her would laugh at such pathetic measures. Her best bet was the man in the next room. Bobby would never let anyone hurt her.

Lucky insisted on joining Jane wherever she went. She couldn't blame the dog. Lucky had been as terrified as Jane when they'd been taken hostage. The dog was now as attached to Bobby as she'd been to her. He had saved them, and neither Jane nor Lucky was ever going to forget that.

Jane stripped off her bloody, dirty, sweaty clothes and tossed them into the trash. She couldn't believe she'd had the wherewithal to throw a second set into her backpack, but she had.

Unwrapping her ankle, she was surprised to discover very little swelling and no pain. Sometimes, if the injury was wrapped quickly and tightly, and it was minor in the first place, no further medical attention was necessary. Her wrist was merely bruised and already on the mend.

The heated water felt heavenly on her body but stung her face. She needed ice to ease the swelling and the ache.

Lucky stuck her head into the shower and a river of mud swirled down the drain.

"You'd better get in here, too," Jane said. "Or there's no way you're sleeping on the bed."

The dog stepped daintily into the tub—sometimes Jane swore Lucky understood everything—and Jane shared the shampoo. Soon they were both squeaky clean, then Jane and Lucky shared the blow dryer.

Jane peered into the mirror, wincing at the sight of her puffy, colorful face. Her mother was going to use this incident to try to convince her to stay in the States. And once again, Jane couldn't let her.

She'd wither and die in D.C. Jane wanted to help the helpless. She needed to be needed. She wasn't happy unless she was working in a country of quiet desperation. The senator had never understood that.

Jane rustled around in her backpack for the extra pair of shorts and tank top she'd stuffed inside. No underwear, no bra, which only made her realize she'd been prancing around the jungle without one.

Thank goodness she hadn't remembered that before now. If she'd known she was bra-less among the sleaze buckets, she'd have been a lot more nervous. As if that were possible.

Come to think of it, none of them had ogled her, sneered, grabbed or behaved in any of the ways she would have expected them to with a helpless woman in their power.

Which was just plain weird and a little bit insulting.

"Idiot," Jane muttered. "Would you have preferred the opposite?"

The idea made her shiver, then she couldn't stop.
She eyed the bed, the blankets, the pillows.

"Just for a minute," she warned herself. "Just to
get warm."

Jane lost the damp towel and slipped beneath the
covers. In an instant she was asleep.

A moment later she began to dream.

CHAPTER SEVEN

FOR DINNER, BOBBY WOULD have preferred steak, baked potatoes and green beans, with a bottle of red wine on the side. What he got was beef and chicken enchiladas, rice, refried beans and tequila.

Beggars couldn't be choosers. When in Rome… et cetera, et cetera. The clichés were as endless as his mother's lectures.

He'd showered while he waited for the food. Managed a phone call to his superior after he'd washed his T-shirt and socks in the sink. The pants he'd just have to wear dirty.

"The woman wasn't kidnapped?" Colonel Delray asked.

"Not when I got here."

"Odd."

"Maybe you should have a talk with the senator."

"Maybe I should."

"And tell her Jane's fine—"

"Jane?" the colonel murmured, amusement as well as warning in his voice.

"Spending twenty-four hours running for your life through the jungle makes short work of titles. Sir."

When on a mission with his team, titles were never used, only first names. In that way, the enemy couldn't find out who was after them, nor which man was in charge. However, Bobby had always had a difficult time calling Delray anything other than "colonel" or "sir."

"Just remember who you are," Delray said. "And who she is."

Bobby frowned. Why had the colonel found it necessary to remind him of that as if he were a kid and unable to keep it in his pants around a female?

Bobby knew the rules. Fraternization with an assignment could get him in huge trouble. But if anyone was worth the trouble—

"The doctor needs sleep," he blurted. "Badly. She shouldn't be disturbed this evening."

"Don't worry, Luchetti, I'll soothe the senator's hysteria. Make sure she doesn't call her daughter, then send a plane in the morning."

"You might want to prepare the senator, as well."

"For?"

Bobby winced at Delray's sharp tone. The colonel was a good soldier, but he hadn't been in the field in a very long time. He didn't remember, or maybe he'd chosen to forget, all that could go wrong with any mission.

"Her daughter's a little banged up."

"*How* little? Dammit, Luchetti, this is a U.S. senator we're talking about. She will eat your liver for lunch when she finds out you let her baby girl be sullied by those monsters."

"Sullied? Oh, no, sir. Nothing like that."

Not that he had any doubts *that* would have followed once they'd gotten the information they wanted. But Jane had kept them at bay—protected him, and in doing so, protected herself.

"*What* then?"

"They hit her."

"How much?"

"Enough. She looks like she ran into a brick wall with her face."

The colonel sighed. "The senator is going to be pissed. Nothing makes 'em madder than when the goods are physically damaged."

"I would think she'd be glad Jane's alive," Bobby said quietly.

"You'd think, wouldn't you?"

Bobby frowned at the spark of annoyance in the colonel's voice. How much of a problem was Senator Harker going to be?

"Put her on the plane, Luchetti."

"Yes, sir."

"Then we'll discuss your next assignment."

"You'll be at Fort Bragg, sir?"

"No. I'll be on the plane."

"What?"

Surprise startled the word out of Bobby without the usual "sir." The colonel didn't appear to notice.

"We're trying to keep this mess under wraps. The senator insists that I be the one to retrieve her daughter. So I'll see you in the morning."

He hung up. Bobby stared at the phone for several seconds. The senator must have a lot of power, or a very big mouth, perhaps both, to warrant this type of treatment.

The food arrived, and Bobby signed for it, then pushed the cart to Jane's door. When he knocked, no one answered.

At first he wasn't concerned. Even when he heard the tiny whimpers, he figured they were Lucky's, imagining the dog on the bed, paws churning as she chased rabbits and squirrels through an imaginary forest.

He was even smiling at the thought, when a cry drifted from inside. Without a moment's hesitation, Bobby lifted his boot and kicked in the door.

JANE'S DREAM WAS LIKE a hundred she'd had before. Someone was dying and she couldn't fix them.

Logically she knew that she was a doctor, not a god. People died. But that didn't mean she had to like, or accept, it.

In this dream, the victim was a child who could have been her own. A cherub with hair much blonder than Jane's and eyes much bluer than the sky. She had...

Jane concentrated, trying to determine what was threatening the child's life. In the way of dreams, she had no concrete answer, only the usual certainty that whatever the disease, there wasn't a thing she could do to help.

The familiar rock of despair settled in her gut, causing her to thrash, moan, then rail against fate, God and modern medicine. For all the good it did.

The exam room receded. The child disappeared, and Jane found herself alone in the middle of a graveyard. She'd had this dream before, too. However, knowing that didn't make the sadness any less oppressive as she walked up and down rows and rows of stones, all marked with the names of her failures.

Glancing around the cemetery, she hoped for someone, anyone, to share her grief, but she was as alone now as she'd been all of her life. Tears pushed at the back of her eyes, a tiny cry escaping before she could shove it back into the darkness where it belonged.

Suddenly there was a loud thud, the bark of a dog, then a large, cool shadow loomed.

She ran, though she had no idea where she was going, no clue where she was. The cemetery had become a jungle. The air had gone so cold she expected flakes of snow to tumble from the dark and threatening sky. Yet no matter where she ran, no matter how fast, someone was right behind her.

When she attempted to call for Bobby, her mouth seemed glued shut. The words stuck in her throat, trapped, bubbling, desperate for a way out, but there was none.

Jane struggled against the night, the silence, the chill, and in the distance someone called her name.

"Help!" she shouted.

The only thing she heard was a muffled plea from lips that still wouldn't open. She tried harder, and the word erupted at last, so loudly she woke up.

The room was dark, but not so dark she couldn't see the man hovering next to the bed. She rocketed upright, and the covers pooled at her waist. The chill of the room made her nipples tighten. She'd fallen asleep without any clothes.

She snatched the sheets to her chest, just as the shadow murmured, "Jane?"

She should have recognized Bobby immediately by the slope of his shoulders, even if she could have ignored Lucky's incredible dance of joy, which was starting to remind her of Snoopy's.

"Are you all right?" he asked.

"Yes." Her hand trembled as she shoved her hair out of her face. "How did you get in?"

He shrugged, the movement telegraphing his embarrassment, and his lack of a shirt. Confused, she glanced toward the thin strand of light coming from the hallway. Her door hung by the hinges.

"What the…?"

Jane searched frantically for evidence of an intruder, but the rest of the room was as shrouded in shadows as Bobby's face.

"I'm sorry," he muttered. "You cried out, but the door was locked."

"You broke down the door?"

"I lost my head."

Jane glanced at the ruined wood, then back at the man. Why did she find the testosterone overload and Neanderthal tactics as attractive as his naked chest? Perhaps because without them, she'd be in a graveyard—and it wouldn't be a dream one.

"Did you have a nightmare?" he pressed.

"Yeah." The details were as clear now as they'd been when she was caught in the grip of that other world. The child, her failure, the graves, someone chasing her. She *hated* those dreams.

Jane's shivers turned into the shakes.

"It's too cold." Bobby turned on the light, then checked the thermostat. "No wonder." He flicked the gauge with his finger. "Busted. You can't sleep in here."

Without waiting for permission, Bobby scooped both her and the bedspread into his arms, then strode out of the room. Though Jane was completely covered, the slide of material between her naked skin and his created a sensation that shot straight to her stomach, then lower. The hard knot of sadness left from her dream dissolved as something else took its place.

"You can't sleep in a room with a broken door." The bed dipped as Bobby sat beside her. "Not in this neighborhood. Not in any neighborhood."

He started to stand, and Jane found herself clinging. The remnants of her dream faded, becoming as ethereal as the scent of Bobby Luchetti and hotel soap.

"Hey." Concern laced his voice. "He'll never hurt you again."

For an instant Jane's mind went blank. Then she understood he was talking about the General.

"It was just a dream," Bobby soothed.

"No."

He stiffened and looked toward the door. "Something more?"

"No." She had a hard time thinking as he tucked her head beneath his chin, and his breath stirred her hair. "I meant I had a dream, but not about him."

"Oh." He sounded confused. "About what, then?"

"Same old, same old."

"Wanna talk about it?"

"Not particularly."

She was used to that nightmare. Psychiatry 101—she felt helpless. She got that. She could no more do anything about the images her subconscious sent than she could about certain types of childhood cancer.

"I suppose you have nightmares, too," she began.

He tensed, and Jane wanted to smack herself. Of *course* he had nightmares. No wonder he rarely slept. She couldn't imagine, and didn't want to, the things he'd seen and done.

"I'm sorry. That's none of my business."

Bobby remained silent, but at least he didn't move away. He was so big, and he poured out heat like a midday sun. Jane was far from small, but next to him she felt almost tiny—protected and cherished. Though she was opening herself to rejection, she burrowed closer and slipped her hand around his waist.

His skin was so warm, smooth, both soft and hard, she couldn't keep her fingers still. She stroked him until, bit by bit, he relaxed, the incredible tension leaving his body even as the chill left hers.

"We should eat," he murmured.

"Not yet."

She didn't want to let him go. He didn't appear to mind. His hands roamed up and down her back in a soothing, rhythmic pattern.

Lucky, bored with the human chatter, jumped onto the other bed, sighed pathetically and lay down.

"I'm sorry I'm being such a…" Jane couldn't think of an adequate word to describe her wussiness.

"Girl?" he supplied.

"Girl?" Her voice sounded a bit shrill. But really. Girl? Was that supposed to be an insult? She couldn't tell.

"Always made my sister crazy when we called her a girl. Even though she was."

"Crazy? Or a girl?"

"Aren't they interchangeable?" She pinched him and Bobby laughed. "Why is it that girls don't like to be girls anymore? What's wrong with being soft, sweet and—"

"What?" Jane whispered.

"Feminine."

"You think I'm…feminine?"

"Oh, yeah."

His voice a sexy rasp in the dark of a tropical night, his hand drifted over the curve of her hip and stayed there.

No one had ever called her feminine. She was too sturdy, too tall. Of course, compared to him, she was neither. She found that notion both intriguing and arousing.

Beneath her palm, his stomach muscles fluttered, and before she could stop herself, she traced the ridges with her thumb.

He caught his breath and the muscles stopped moving. His fingers tightened on her hip, drawing her closer. His hands no longer comforting, they were also no longer on the other side of the sheet but on her skin. She didn't mind.

Though she hadn't dreamed about the general and his thugs, hadn't yet rehashed every minute in their company, that didn't mean she wouldn't if given the chance. Jane didn't want that chance; she wanted this one, with Bobby. If he was here, she wouldn't have any more bad dreams. A foolish belief, but she clung to it, nevertheless, even as she clung to him.

"Don't—" she began, and he snatched his hand back as if she'd suddenly exploded in flames.

"Stop," she finished.

Bobby started to inch away. She clenched her fingers around his biceps and held on.

"Don't stop," she whispered. "Don't go. Don't leave me. Not tonight."

He hesitated, and she played her last card, inching back just enough so the sheet slithered to her waist. He froze, his gaze locked on her breasts, fascinated, as if he'd never seen any before.

Reaching out, he stroked first one, then the other, before lifting his eyes to hers. For the first time since he'd come to her rescue, he looked at her face, and he didn't flinch at the sight of the bruises.

His hands were big enough to hold her in his palms, rough enough to excite her with a simple touch. Stark against her skin, their masculinity an intriguing contrast to her feminine curves.

He stared into her face, but little glances below her neck revealed what he was really interested in. Since she'd never had a man so fascinated with any part of her, not even her mind, she wasn't sure what to do. She *was* sure that his timid touch excited her more than she believed such things could.

"This is such a bad idea," he murmured.

"Seems like a good one to me."

"There are things you don't know—"

"I don't want to." She took a deep breath and admitted the truth. "I just want you."

He blinked. No doubt he'd never met a woman so forward. Or maybe so desperate.

Her face heated; she was terrified he'd turn her down. She almost jumped up and ran back to her room, then he smiled, touched her face and whispered, "Me, too."

Pushing her back on the bed, he slid his fingers over her with a reverence she wouldn't have believed he could possess. Her eyes drifted closed as she waited for the heat of his mouth on her breast, the moist flicker of a tongue along her nipple.

Instead, his lips brushed her abdomen. Her eyes flashed open as he traced a moist path to her navel, then took a fold of her skin between his teeth and suckled.

The sight of his dark head at her belly, his mouth

against her, made her shift with uneasy excitement. His palm cupped her hip again, holding her still, and he glanced all the way up her body.

"I've been wanting to taste you, right here—" he pressed his lips to the fluttering muscles of her stomach "—since you tore apart your shirt."

She'd thought he was fixated on her breasts. She had to admit they weren't bad, but they're weren't big. Didn't guys like big?

What difference did it make? Especially when he was practically worshipping her in ways she'd never imagined could be so erotic.

His eyes glittered in the tiny bit of light, reminding her of the times his gaze had drifted over her belly and made her yearn. She'd been longing to put her mouth on his skin almost since he'd taken away her knife. She tried to sit up so she could touch him, but when her stomach muscles flexed he rode them with his thumb, ran his tongue along the wave, and she forgot what she'd been about to do.

"Let me," he whispered, his breath brushing the path left by his tongue and making her shiver.

He memorized her dips and curves. She had to touch him or explode, put her mouth on him or die.

Intent on learning the flavor of his skin, she bumped her lip on his bicep, and when she tasted him, she tasted blood. Horrified, she pulled back, staring at the dark streak that marred his arm.

For an instant she thought he was hurt and she hadn't even known. Then she realized her lip had begun to bleed again. Jane frantically wiped at the mark, but Bobby grabbed her hand, stilling her movements.

"I've seen blood before, Jane. You have, too. Forget it."

He brushed her hair from her face, then used a corner of the sheet to gently blot the sting from her lips.

"No more kisses for you," he whispered, and when she pouted, he laughed. "But that doesn't mean none for me."

Lowering his head, he kissed from her neck down to her toes. She was tingling by the time he was through, then he showed her that he'd only just begun.

Being unable to kiss was strange, making the encounter less personal, somehow. No kissing made this all about sex, and while that should bother her, amazingly, it didn't.

She'd nearly died, several times over. Would anything ever bother her again?

"You're thinking too much." Bobby pressed his mouth to the line that must have appeared between her eyebrows. The one her mother said was making her look old.

Whoa! She didn't want to think about her mother right now. Talk about a mood killer!

"Sorry," she murmured, letting her hands drift over his back, his arms, his chest.

He had such beautiful skin, with such big muscles rippling beneath. She could spend a week—and she'd like to—learning everything about his incredible body.

"Don't be sorry."

His mouth grazed her temple. His erection pushed against his jeans and brushed her stomach. She wanted to pull him close and hold him inside of her forever.

Reaching between them, she traced a fingertip up the solid ridge. His breath caught and he stilled. Cupping him through the material, she discovered his muscles weren't the only big thing about him.

She tugged at the button. "Off."

"Jane, I don't—"

"Do." She used her fingernail on him again, tracing a line parallel to his zipper. The darkness made her bold; the need made her brave.

"Do me," she whispered as she worked his jeans open and slipped her fingers inside.

Hot and smooth, he pulsed in her palm. Somehow he managed to kick off his pants with very little help. She supposed he'd been trained for just about anything.

She spent some time getting to know him. Hands instead of mouth, skin to skin, her entire body hummed as it called out to his. Guiding him to her, he came without hesitation. Sliding inside, he made her feel...

She wasn't sure of the exact word beyond *better*. He made her feel better.

She'd always considered sex a normal physical function performed between consenting adults. Not that she'd consented all that often. But when she had, she'd been satisfied. She'd always wanted to do it again. Maybe not right at that moment, but eventually.

After tonight, she'd want to do it all the time. With him. And that was a very dangerous thing to want. He couldn't stay. Neither could she. This was about attraction, lust, life, nothing more, and she had to remember that.

So she focused on sensation, the brush of his leg against hers, the hardness of his hip along her belly, the drift of his mouth on her neck and his fingers in her hair.

How could she be both tense and relaxed at the same time, both energized yet lulled?

The scent of his skin was familiar. Had she only known him a few days? He filled her so completely, touched her so tenderly, held her so tightly, she felt as if they'd already shared a lifetime.

When he murmured her name and pressed his lips to the frown line between her eyes, she tightened around him, drawing both his release and her own.

His shadow rose above her, wide and strong. She was trapped by his weight, surrounded by his hands, pinned by his body. But she knew she was safe.

Instead of running from the room and her life, he stayed right where he was, as if he didn't want to leave the shelter of her body any more than she wanted him to. The behavior went a long way toward soothing the sudden fear that he'd slept with her out of pity.

"What happened?" he muttered.

"And here I'd thought you'd done this before. Port in every storm? Or is that a girl in every port?"

"You're thinking of the navy, and I'm not like that."

"Like what?"

"I don't sleep around. Much," he qualified. "I've never been good at it."

"I have to disagree. You're very good at it."

"I—we—" He broke off with an exasperated sigh and let his forehead touch hers. "This wasn't about gratitude, was it?"

"What?"

"A thank-you-for-saving-my-life boink?"

"You think I'd—"

She couldn't finish the sentence. She'd been worried about pity, and he was worried about payback.

"Did you?" he asked quietly.

She ran her hand over his hair. "I *am* grateful. For my life and the sex. But one had nothing to do with the other. I promise. I wanted you. I needed this."

"Me, too," he murmured.

"Then relax. Sleep. Okay?"

He rolled to the side but captured her fingers as he did so, making the movement more about staying than going.

"Okay," he whispered.

CHAPTER EIGHT

BOBBY AWOKE TO SEVERAL realizations. The sun was shining in his eyes. He was alone in bed. He'd done exactly what the colonel warned him *not* to do, and he hadn't used a condom while doing it.

"Shit."

"Excuse me?"

Jane stuck her head out of the bathroom. Bobby turned in that direction and came nose to snout with Lucky. She kissed him, right on the mouth.

"Ack!"

He rubbed his face on the pillow. Even when the slobber was gone, he still felt contaminated.

Jane laughed. "For a man who's spent eons in countries without plumbing, you're awfully picky about dog germs."

"Yeah, I'm funny that way." He sat up, resting his head in his hands as he tried to figure out how to tell Jane he'd screwed up.

"Headache?" she asked. "I'm afraid I don't have any aspirin handy."

"I didn't have a condom handy, either."

The silence of the room was broken by Lucky's

joyful panting, which only seemed to exaggerate Bobby's unjoyous announcement.

When he couldn't stand the quiet anymore, Bobby raised his head, prepared for Jane's expression of horror. Instead she stared at him as if she could see everything about him—even the things he didn't want her to.

"It's all right," she said.

"No, it isn't. Dammit, Jane, I didn't even think about protection until right now."

"Neither did I." She gave a small smile. "I could only think of you."

He groaned and fell back on the bed, throwing his arm over his face. Not only was he a pig, but an irresponsible one at that. How could he have slept with Jane? Sadly, it had been all too easy.

Jane crossed the room, and the bed dipped as she sat next to him.

"It's all right," she repeated. "I'm on the pill. I have to be."

Bobby dropped his arm and met her gaze. "Have to?"

"In my line of work, there's no telling when I might be assaulted. Birth control pills are issued along with immunizations when we leave home."

"You're on the pill in case you're raped?" His fingers curled into fists.

"Better safe than sorry."

She didn't appear concerned. He was terrified. "Why on earth do you do this job?"

Jane lifted her eyebrows. "The same reason you do yours. I can help."

"And every day you live with the threat of violence?"

"Don't you?"

"Yeah, but—"

"You're a man, so it's okay?"

"I didn't say that."

"What did you say?"

A sudden urge to pull her close and protect her forever nearly overwhelmed him. An uncommon urge, one he'd never had before. Not even with Marlie. The thought confused him so much he was dizzy with it.

Bobby took a deep breath, let it out slowly until the dizziness passed. Unfortunately the confusion remained.

"Pregnancy isn't the only issue we need to deal with," he pointed out.

"I was tested for every disease known to man before I came to Mexico. Since I've been here," she lifted one shoulder, then lowered it. "Well, let's just say I'm clean."

Bobby thought about the physical he'd just taken, the condoms he'd *always* used—until last night. "Me, too."

"Nothing to worry about, then." She bounced to her feet and headed for the bathroom.

He watched her go, amazed, fascinated and just a little dazzled. Maybe they were bound by danger. Maybe what had happened had created an emotional attachment between them—one that would disappear when the danger did.

Nevertheless, she was special and he wanted her to know that.

"You're the bravest woman I've ever met," he blurted.

The door closed behind Jane. Bobby wasn't even sure she'd heard him.

"I'M NOT," SHE WHISPERED to her reflection. "I'm a chicken-livered, yellow-bellied coward."

Jane searched through her backpack, but she knew what she'd find. Or rather wouldn't.

Birth control pills.

She hadn't exactly had the time to retrieve them before Bobby hustled her out of the hut. The worst part was she hadn't had the guts to tell him. She'd lied—by omission certainly, but a lie just the same.

"The chances he got me pregnant last night are pretty damn slim," she told the mirror.

They always are, her reflection answered.

Jane turned on the shower and let the tepid water wash the sleep from her eyes. Too bad it couldn't wash away the sense of guilt.

She wrestled with that guilt as she washed first her hair, then her body. Stepping out, she grabbed a towel.

"No reason to tell him until I know for certain that I'm—"

Screwed? the voice from the mirror interrupted.

Jane chose to ignore that voice.

A tap sounded on the door. "You okay?" Bobby called. "I thought I heard you talking."

"I'm fine."

"We need to get to the plane."

"I'll be there in a minute."

After today, she'd never see Bobby Luchetti again. The thought brought a wave of sadness so strong her eyes burned.

"Idiot," she muttered.

She'd been a one-night stand. For that matter, so had he. No reason to get all sentimental. Those who got sentimental about a man only got hurt.

She was smarter than that. Sex but no relationship. Child but no husband. She had a plan, remember? A plan that didn't include soldier boy any more than his plans included her.

Jane stepped from the bathroom fully dressed to find Bobby right outside. Figuring he wanted the shower, she tried to scoot past. He captured her fingers with his and stared into her battered face. She knew what he saw. Though it didn't seem possible, she looked worse today than yesterday.

"One more thing," he said.

Her heart sped up. Foolish, foolish heart.

"Yes?"

Why was her voice so breathy and faint? Thankfully, Bobby didn't seem to notice.

"We should keep this to ourselves."

"This?"

"This." He indicated the rumpled bed. Her. Him. "It could be a problem."

"Problem?"

When had she become a parrot?

"I shouldn't have slept with an assignment."

Jane stiffened. An assignment? She'd known she was a one-nighter, but an assignment? That stung.

Bobby tightened his fingers around hers. "Not that I'm sorry. But—"

"You could get in trouble."

"Yeah. And I doubt it would do you much good, either."

"Me?"

"We're from two different worlds, Jane. You're a senator's daughter. I'm a farmer's son. Doctor." He pointed to her, then to himself. "Soldier."

"Indian chief," she muttered.

"You don't think it would matter, but it would. Besides, there are things you don't know about me—"

He'd said that last night, but she'd been too interested in his body to listen.

A sad, faraway expression crossed his face, and her stomach dropped to her feet, leaving an icy lump of disgust in its wake. He'd said he wasn't married, but—

"You're engaged."

"What?" His startled gaze returned to hers. "No. Never. Guys like me…we don't get married, Jane. We do get divorced quite often, though."

"You're divorced?"

"No." He kissed her brow. "And I don't plan to be. I'm better off alone. I just forgot that for a while."

He went into the bathroom and closed the door. She stared at it until she heard the shower come on.

Why did she feel as if he were trying to convince himself as much as her?

And why would she need convincing? She didn't want to get married. Great sex didn't change that.

A half an hour later, Jane and Bobby stepped onto the airport tarmac, where a private plane idled. Lucky trotted at Jane's heels as if she were on parade.

Though he was as rumpled as she was, Bobby still managed to appear stiff and proper as he escorted Jane to the waiting aircraft. He held her elbow in a formal grip. She wanted to run back and hide forever in the stuffy hotel room with the lumpy bed.

A man emerged from the cabin. He was tall and lean, and his hair, or what was left of it, had faded to white. His face was tanned, lined, lived-in. Though he wore a dark suit and not a uniform, he still held himself in a way that revealed he'd once been on the edge, and could be again if the situation warranted it. Since Bobby saluted him, she figured the man held a rank higher than captain.

"Luchetti. Nice work."

Bobby started and Jane glanced at him. But his face remained impassive as he said, "Thank you, sir."

"Ma'am, I'm Colonel Delray. Your mother sent me to bring you home."

Knowing Mother, she'd given him explicit instructions, which no doubt included hog-tying Jane if she made any noises about returning to the jungle.

"Captain, if you'd escort Dr. Harker to her seat, I'll wait to speak with you here."

Bobby moved forward; Jane hung back. "Speak with you about what?"

Bobby flicked a glance at the colonel, who gave a slight nod. "He's my superior officer."

Jane blinked. "My mother not only sent a Delta Force operator after me, she sent his superior?"

The colonel frowned.

Oops. Maybe she wasn't supposed to know Bobby was Delta. Well, too bad. This had gone beyond ridiculous and into bizarre.

"Your mother was concerned," the colonel said.

"No doubt. How embarrassing for the senior senator from Rhode Island to have a daughter kidnapped by drug dealers in the jungle."

"She loves you."

Jane snorted, earning twin expressions of shock from the men, which she ignored.

The colonel's eyes bugged at the sight of Lucky. "What's that?"

"Don't even think about telling me I can't take her on the plane," Jane snapped. "I am in *no* mood."

"Your mother will not be pleased."

"She never is."

Jane and Lucky trotted up the steps and into the plane with Bobby at their heels. The interior reminded her of *Austin Powers*. The only thing missing was the revolving bed.

"Cushy," she commented. "Wonder who she borrowed this from. And what she had to promise to use it."

Bobby hovered near the entrance, all stiff and at

attention. Lucky slobbered on his knee, and when he didn't acknowledge the love, she trotted over to collapse in a heap of skin and fur at Jane's feet.

"What's the matter?" she asked.

"You're different."

"Thanks," she muttered.

"I mean you're acting differently. Hard. Cold. You don't like your mother. It's…disturbing."

"I *love* my mother."

"But you don't *like* her."

"Wait until you meet her. You won't like her, either."

"I doubt I'll be meeting her."

Bobby glanced out the door, lifted a hand in acknowledgment. "I have to go. So do you."

This was goodbye. Forever. Jane wasn't ready.

She muttered, "Stay," to the dog. Not that she had to. Lucky was already out cold. She'd had a busy night sleeping.

Jane should be tired; instead she was hyperalert. She wanted to do this goodbye right—not too clingy, not too stilted. How did one say goodbye to a man you didn't want to say goodbye to?

Bobby took two quick steps into the cabin and nearly slammed into Jane as she headed toward him. At first she thought he was eager to touch her, then she realized he didn't want the colonel to see them.

Stopping a mere breath away, he stared into her face. "This will pass."

"What?" she whispered.

"This." He brushed a knuckle across her bruised cheek. "I've had a few. They don't last."

Jane had nearly forgotten about her face. How could she have? The colonel hadn't commented, which was odd, unless you considered he'd seen a hundred more just like hers. And wasn't that a cheery thought?

Jane inched closer until their bodies aligned. She laid her palms on his chest. "Bobby, I—"

She stopped, uncertain what to say.

Don't go.

Come with me.

"I like you." The words slipped out. She felt herself blush and ducked her head.

He lifted her chin with a finger. "Ditto."

"Luchetti!"

The colonel's shout made them both spring away from each other. Lucky grumbled; their guilty movements had woken her up.

"If you ever need…" He shrugged.

"Rescuing?"

"Yeah."

"You'll be the first person I call."

They stared at each other, neither one of them sure what to do. How ridiculous. She'd shared her body with this man only a few hours before, and now she couldn't figure out the proper etiquette for goodbye. No wonder she was more at home in the jungle.

"Bye," she whispered.

He gathered her into his arms and she went gladly. He was so strong, so warm, so…Bobby. She hugged him tightly, and his lips brushed her hair.

"So long."

Bobby inched back, and she fought not to cling,

even when he seemed to, dragging his hands down her arms, allowing his fingers to tangle with hers before falling away to hang loosely at his sides.

He executed a sharp turn and marched out the door. Only then did Jane realize he'd never once kissed her on the lips.

His boots clattered down the steps. Lucky whined pathetically.

"I know exactly how you feel, girl."

THE COLONEL STOOD AT the bottom of the gangway. His sharp brown eyes peered into Bobby's as if searching for an answer. But what was the question?

"Well?" he prompted. "What happened with the senator's daughter?"

How could the man know everything all the time when he wasn't even there?

"I can explain."

Bobby's mind raced. He needed to make this good enough to avoid a reprimand. Hell, he'd better hope he could avoid a court martial. If the senator wanted to get testy about his night of passion with her daughter, she could make life mighty uncomfortable for a man like Bobby.

"Get to it," the colonel said. "Why was the doctor not kidnapped when you got here, then kidnapped as soon as you were?"

Bobby blinked. His boss wasn't asking about the sex—no kidding—he was asking about the mission.

"I don't understand it, either, sir."

Bobby proceeded to explain the oddities in the situation. When he was through, the colonel remained silent for several seconds.

"Makes no sense at all. I'll have another talk with Senator Harker."

"What did she say when she first contacted you?"

"There was a call saying her daughter had been kidnapped."

"And on that you sent me?"

Delray shrugged. "She's a senator. She insisted."

Well, Bobby had been sent worse places on less intel. That was the nature of his job.

"Until we know what's what," the colonel continued, "she'll be safer in D.C."

Bobby had his doubts she'd be any safer in D.C., but he wasn't supposed to make the plans, only implement them.

"Your men are off Bowstring for a few more weeks?" the colonel asked.

Delta squadrons rotated on and off Bowstring in thirty-day increments. When on, they resided at Fort Bragg, ready to go anywhere, for anything, at a moment's notice while updating their counterterrorism training. When off Bowstring, Delta operators traveled.

"Yes, sir. Some are at language school. A few on arctic instruction."

Delray snorted. "As if they'll be using *that* anytime soon."

Bobby agreed, but they needed to be ready, nevertheless.

"Since you've got some time," the colonel continued, "and you don't mind Mexico—"

Bobby wasn't all that fond of the country, but then he hadn't been fond of Afghanistan, Pakistan or Iraq, either. That didn't mean he couldn't work there.

He should probably take a leave and head home as he'd promised. But after the fiasco with Colin and Marlie, going home and either being babied or teased, probably both, held very little appeal.

"I don't mind," he blurted.

"Great. Hang around a few days. See what you can dig up. This entire scenario bugs the living hell out of me. Let me know what you find out."

"Where will you be, sir?"

"Washington." Colonel Delray scowled. "I'm helping the senator put together a request to increase funding for Delta."

Which explained why the colonel was dallying in Washington rather than heading to Fort Bragg where he belonged. It also explained why he was taking orders from a politician. He'd do anything to benefit Delta.

Colonel Delray started up the gangway at a brisk pace. When he reached the top, he nodded farewell, then the door closed behind him, and the plane pulled away.

Bobby stared at the windows, but Jane never materialized. He watched until the aircraft was no more than a dot in the bright blue Mexican sky before he left and went to work.

He filled his canteen, bought some food and another set of clothing, then changed and walked back into the jungle. He'd thought he was heartily sick of sand countries. He'd wanted to see a few trees. But as the vegetation closed in around him and the humidity pressed against his skin, starting a low headache at the base of his skull, Bobby almost missed the grit of sand in his teeth.

Almost. What he really missed was Jane. Funny, but it was lonely here without her. And that wasn't funny at all.

Why was he still thinking about Jane? He was in love with Marlie. How could he pine for one woman, then have sex with another?

Bobby cursed. He had to quit thinking about both of them. Being distracted by a female was a good way to get killed.

He headed for the hut where the Little General had died. Though Bobby hadn't had time to do much reconnaissance then, he planned on doing a helluva lot now. Then he'd trot over to the airfield and finish at the village.

However, when he reached the hut, all of the bodies were gone. And not just dragged away or buried in the jungle gone. But *gone* gone. As if they'd never been there.

No blood. No bullets. No freaking hut. The thing had been blown up.

"At least I know where my demolition went."

He was talking to himself again.

Bobby zipped his lip and hiked toward the airfield. He found the same thing—a smoking gully where there'd once been a building, and no bodies.

Unease trickled over him, and Bobby double-timed it back to the first place he'd ever seen Jane.

By then night had fallen. A dog woofed, a child whined. The people were still there; so were the huts. Except for hers. That one had been burned to a crisp. Jane was not going to be happy when she sent for her medical books and instruments.

"What the hell?" Bobby muttered.

He took one step out of the woods and a bullet thunked into the tree behind him. Hitting the ground, he reached for his weapon.

No outcry was raised. Either everyone was deaf to gunfire, or they were *glad* one of their own was trying to kill an American soldier.

Since dead American soldiers always caused huge amounts of trouble, Bobby was betting gunfire was so commonplace in this part of Quintana Roo, no one cared.

Bobby crouched at the edge of the village, thinking. Bad guys had stolen, then used, his demolition to eliminate any hint that both he and Jane had been here. Why?

They'd kidnapped Jane, then questioned her about *him*. Again why?

Now Jane was gone, Bobby was here, and someone was trying to kill him. Again.

He was so damn sick of being shot at.

The realization made him pause. When had that happened? While he'd never enjoyed the sensation of a bullet whizzing past his cheek, he'd never wanted to rip off the shooter's head before.

Of course, this guy was most likely one of those who'd tried to kill them in the jungle. An action that had led to Jane being kidnapped and hurt.

The memory of Jane's battered face made him wince. Though she'd insisted she hadn't relived the beating in her dreams, he had a bad feeling she would eventually. How could she not?

The longing to be with her when that happened was so overwhelming, Bobby had to force himself to remain where he was instead of running to Puerto and hopping the next plane to D.C.

What he needed now was one of the bad guys to extract information from.

So Bobby continued his stealthy reconnaissance of the village.

CHAPTER NINE

WITHIN TEN MINUTES, Bobby found the shooter; five minutes later the guy was disarmed, disabled and ready to blab everything he knew. Then it took only ten minutes more to convince the man he could speak English just fine.

"Why did you try to kill the American doctor?"

"Money."

"Who paid you?"

Bobby clenched his fists. The man saw the movement and hurried to tell him.

"Someone who is great friends with Armando Escobar."

Escobar was the nastiest up-and-coming drug dealer in southern Mexico. What did he have against Jane?

"The man you killed in the jungle?" his captive continued.

"Which one?"

"The leader."

Ah-ha. The General.

"What about him?"

"Killing him was a mistake. He is important to Escobar."

"Not anymore."

"For always. The man was his son."

That wasn't good. Drug lords became extremely annoyed when Special Forces operatives killed their sons. Bobby could hardly blame them. However, if they'd stop sending their children on missions to beat and terrorize women, such things wouldn't happen.

"What does Escobar want with Dr. Harker?"

"If he wanted her, he wouldn't kill her."

"Why does he want her dead?"

"He doesn't."

Bobby's headache was getting worse. He'd never had any patience with interrogation. Which was why he usually left it to the CIA.

"Explain," he growled.

"Someone else wants her dead."

"Who?"

"I do not know." His gaze darted to the side, then back.

"You know *something*." Bobby drew his sidearm. The action was usually all it took to make amateurs blab even more. This man was no exception.

"I overheard Enrique say a rich American wanted the doctor killed, and in such a way as to send a message."

"To who?"

"I do not know. Truly."

That double tap to the head had always bothered

Bobby. It was a hit, plain and simple. But why? What had Jane ever done but help people?

"A message," he murmured, as the puzzle pieces started to slide together in some semblance of sense.

If Jane was dead, she wasn't getting any message. But someone else would be. And who would be the one most likely to need convincing of something?

Bobby cursed. No wonder Senator Harker had sent him down here. She was being blackmailed with her daughter's life.

Jane wasn't safe in Washington. Jane wasn't safe anywhere. Except with him. Maybe.

"You'd better get out of the country, *amigo*. Escobar is after you."

"Him and half the Middle East."

"I would not make light. The man is…"

"What?"

"*Loco.* He has sampled too much of his own product."

Just what Bobby needed. An up-and-coming drug dealer with cocaine dementia who wanted him dead because he'd killed his son.

But Escobar had to catch him first, which was going to be difficult. By this time tomorrow, Bobby planned to be glued to Jane's side in Washington, D.C.

JANE'S PLANE MADE A WIDE turn and began its approach to Ronald Reagan Airport. From her window, she observed various national landmarks stretching toward the sky.

Since 9/11, whenever she flew into Washington, Jane got the chills. Her generation was fated to remember what they'd been doing at the exact moment those planes had hit the World Trade Center and the Pentagon, just as her mother's generation remembered what they'd been doing when they heard Kennedy was shot.

Jane had been at her mother's condo. She'd flown in the day before, just as she was flying in now, but that time she'd been returning from Brazil.

She'd climbed into the limo her mother had sent and traveled past the Pentagon. A single day later she might have been one of the people who'd stopped on the bridge, disturbed by the seriously low-flying jet.

Where had Bobby been on that fateful morning in September? Wherever he was, she had no doubt he'd hopped the first transport to Afghanistan.

Where was he now?

Jane sighed. What was it about D.C. that made her nostalgic, nervous and just a little bit sad?

Oh, yeah. Her mother.

Jane glanced out the window as the plane taxied toward a waiting limousine. Lucky grumbled from her window seat.

"Wait until you meet her," Jane murmured. "Then we can really have a discussion."

"Doctor?" Colonel Delray exited the cockpit, where he'd hidden for the entire trip. His dark eyes skimmed her bruised face. "Let me talk to her first."

"Be my guest."

With a nod of approval, Delray headed for the

door, which seemed to open miraculously at an imperious flick of his hand. He glanced outside and cringed.

"Let me guess," Jane said. "She's on her way up."

The colonel's rueful shrug revealed he'd dealt with the senator before. Jane braced herself for the whirlwind that was Raeanne Harker.

"Jane," the senator snapped the instant she set foot in the cabin. "We need to do some damage control."

Though Raeanne Harker stood just over five feet two inches, she exuded the confidence of a much larger woman. Slim and patrician, blond, of course, she was beautiful, smart, rich and powerful. Raeanne wouldn't settle for anything less.

Which might be one of the reasons Jane's refusal to fall into line drove her batty.

"Too late, mother dearest."

Raeanne frowned. "I've told you not to call me that."

"You've told me a lot of things. I rarely listen."

Jane's mother looked at her for the first time, and her heavily lashed, violet eyes widened. She muttered an expletive that would have been bleeped on every major television news show. When Raeanne got angry, she could win a cursing contest with any dockworker in America.

That she was rarely able to indulge only seemed to make her cursing, when she did it, more profound. In truth, Raeanne's trash mouth was one of the few things Jane liked about her. When she swore, she seemed almost human.

"Dammit, Delray! What the hell is this?"

Raeanne stalked over to Jane and went on tiptoe to take a good look at her black-and-blue face.

Delray motioned to the attendant. The man quietly shut the outer door, then slid into the cockpit.

"I thought I was your daughter." Jane turned away.

Her mother grabbed her elbow and yanked Jane back. Lucky growled, a rumble that rippled along Jane's spine like nails across a chalkboard. Not Lucky's drug-dealer snarl, but close.

Raeanne glanced toward the dog and cursed again. "What's that?"

Jane pointed to herself. "Daughter." Then to Lucky. "Dog. Repeat after me."

"Don't be a smart-ass, Jane. You can't go out in public with your face so beat up. What were you thinking?"

Jane couldn't help it. She laughed.

While the senator might curse like the Little General, there the comparison ended. Her mother didn't slap her around to make her shut up. What a great mom.

"The guy who did this didn't care how bad I'd look in the morning since he planned on burying me in a shallow Mexican grave. I'm sorry it's going to inconvenience you on the evening news, but I didn't want to come here. Your toady insisted."

The colonel's eyes narrowed at being referred to as a toady, but he didn't say a word, which only proved he was exactly that.

"Suite at the Jefferson," her mother said, naming the newest hotel for the elite, located just a few blocks from the White House. "Have the plastic surgeon meet us there."

"Mother, I do *not* need a plastic surgeon."

"What do you know about it?"

"I'm a doctor!" Jane shouted.

The plane went silent.

Shouting at her mother never did any good. Jane had learned that while still a teenager.

Taking a deep breath, she tried again. "There's nothing broken. The bruises will fade. I want to get back to Mexico and do my job."

"Like hell," Raeanne muttered.

"Why did you insist I be brought here? And why did you tell—" Jane glanced at the colonel "—*them* that I was kidnapped?"

"You were."

"Not until *after* Bobby showed up."

"Bobby?"

"Captain Luchetti," the colonel interjected. "One of my best."

Raeanne gave a sharp nod. Of course they'd sent the best. Otherwise they would have answered to her.

"There was a threat. How was I supposed to know they called before they did the deed?"

Jane frowned. There was something off about that logic. But she wasn't quite sure what.

"What, exactly, did they say?"

"That you had been kidnapped."

"Then why were they trying to kill me?"

Her mother looked away. "How am I supposed to know what sets off a Mexican thug? I'm just happy you're here and it's over."

"It's not over if someone still wants me dead."

"Let Delray deal with that."

Her mother's answer to everything. Delegate.

"If you had a cell phone," Raeanne continued, "I could have called and checked on you."

"I hate cell phones," Jane muttered. Mainly because her mother was always calling her on them.

"Enter the modern world, Jane. Everyone has a cell phone."

To Jane that merely meant everyone needed their heads examined.

"Let's get you to the hotel."

Raeanne began to walk toward the entrance and *bam,* the attendant reappeared and opened the door. Must be nice to live on Fantasy Island.

"Mother, I have a job. People who need me."

"I need you. Can't you spend a few days with your mother? At least until your face heals. At least until we figure out what's going on."

Jane hesitated. She wanted to go back to Mexico, not only because she liked it—or at least she had until the whole Enrique-trying-to-kill-her incident—but Bobby was there. Maybe she'd run into him again in the jungle.

The stupidity of that hope made her snort derisively, earning an admonishing glare from her mother.

"It would be foolish to return to Quintana Roo

when we don't know who's trying to kill you," the colonel added.

He had a point. Nevertheless...

"I can't stay here indefinitely."

"Of course not," Raeanne wheedled. "A few days. You can relax. Get a pedicure, some highlights."

Jane resisted the urge to roll her eyes. As if a salon session would make everything better.

Then again, it couldn't hurt.

"All right," she allowed. "A few days."

Raeanne graced Jane with a rare smile. After all, she *was* getting her way.

"You take the limo, Jane. Colonel. I'll take a cab back to the Hill."

"You aren't going with me?" Jane asked, surprised.

"It's the middle of the day. Why on earth would I go with you?"

Jane sighed. Why should her near-death experience change anything?

"Let's go, Lucky."

"That *thing* is not going to the Jefferson." Raeanne stood at the top of the gangway staring at the dog with an expression of such disgust Jane feared she might pop a wrinkle.

"That *thing* is Lucky and she goes where I go." Jane gazed first at her mother, then at the colonel. "Nonnegotiable. She's saved my life more than anyone else ever has."

"I doubt the concierge at the Jefferson will be impressed."

"People bring their yappy dogs there all the time. I'm sure Paris Hilton lets her Chihuahua sleep right on the bed."

Although she doubted Paris stayed at the Jefferson; she'd stay at a Hilton, wouldn't she? But that was beside the point.

"Maybe if I dress Lucky in a…dress, they'll allow her to come in."

"God, no," Raeanne muttered. "That would be too frightening."

"Make it happen, Mother." Jane scooted past her, then down the steps and into the limo.

By the time they reached the Jefferson everything was arranged. Though Jane sneered at her mother's imperious manner, her prima donna expectations, they did make life so much simpler.

Jane was hustled through the back entrance like a celebrity. Why was it that whenever she walked through an industrial kitchen she thought of Bobby Kennedy?

Uneasy, Jane glanced around the shiny chrome showplace. But no one lurked in the shadows with a gun. They were all too busy preparing for the lunch rush.

The colonel ushered her into an unassuming elevator tucked into a hallway behind the walk-in freezers.

"The penthouse?" Jane murmured, as he used a security key to access the top floor.

"Has the entire floor to itself and an elevator all its own. Easiest place to defend."

"Defend from what?"

The door slid open, and Jane stepped into the most beautiful suite with the most beautiful view she'd ever seen. Fresh flowers graced glass tables, bottles with liquor in every shade of brown—caramel, amber, topaz—lined a cherry-wood bar backed with mirrors.

Enchanted, Jane walked across the marble foyer, to stand at a bank of windows on the other side. The city of Washington, D.C., spread out before her like a banquet. She'd never much cared for the place, but when observed from this far up, Jane had to admit it was lovely.

When she turned around, Lucky had already climbed onto a couch the shade of eggshells and fallen asleep. The elevator doors began to close, and Delray lifted a hand in goodbye without ever answering her question.

Jane showered and tied the thick white hotel robe around her waist, then ordered room service. She had a pedicure and a massage, before a maid dropped off new clothes.

It was only when she tried to take Lucky for a walk and discovered the guard in the elevator waiting to do the job for her, that Jane realized she was as much of a prisoner now as she'd been in the hut with the Little General.

GETTING OUT OF MEXICO proved more difficult than Bobby had thought. Escobar was indeed after him, and the man wasn't a fool. Before Bobby had walked a hundred yards from the village, he heard an outcry, and he was on the run.

He probably should have killed the guy he'd questioned, but the man had done nothing but follow orders. Bobby had a hard time shooting people for doing the same thing he did, even if they were on the other side.

Bobby escaped, or at least he made them think that he had, then he circled back, listened to their conversation, even deciphered some of it.

Half wait here, half head to Puerto. Kill the American soldier.

Bobby stifled a curse. He was supposed to be extracted from Puerto tomorrow. Now what?

He improvised, something he'd been good at even before Delta training, making a beeline through the jungle. Sleeping little, eating less, he reached the Gulf coast in three days, leaving Escobar's men waiting for him on the wrong side of the country.

From there it was a simple matter to call for a pickup. He could have phoned the colonel, told him what he'd learned, but the idea made Bobby nervous.

Someone in Washington was involved in the attempt on Jane's life, he was certain of it. Knowing Washington, that someone was tapping every phone they could find. Better to go there himself, brief his boss, then find Jane.

That he was rationalizing wasn't lost on Bobby. He wanted to see her. Period.

Though he tried not to analyze his behavior, he couldn't help it. He had far too much time to think.

Lust wasn't anything new to him, but lusting for an assignment was. He had to conclude he was on the rebound.

Jane had wanted him, and Bobby hadn't realized how much he needed to be wanted. He shouldn't have slept with her, and now that he had, he should let her go.

Only thing was, he couldn't do it.

Bobby reached D.C. four days after Jane should have. He phoned the colonel and was instructed to head to the Pentagon. There the two men commandeered a conference room, and Bobby told his superior everything. Or almost.

"A message," the colonel murmured. "To the senator. I'll have to talk to her. Again."

"In the meantime—" Bobby stood, anxious to get to Jane "—I'll protect Dr. Harker."

"Unnecessary." The colonel waved his hand as if Bobby were a pesky bug. "She's being well protected."

"But—"

The colonel lifted a brow. "But, what?"

"I believe I can protect her the best, sir."

"You always do."

"I'd like to at least talk to her."

"No."

Bobby blinked. "What?"

"You've taken SERE training. You know that kidnapping victims can attach to their rescuers as well as their kidnappers. It's better if Dr. Harker never sees you again."

Was that what had happened between him and Jane? Nothing more than a case of rescuer worship? Could be. Made as much sense as anything else. Nevertheless, he wasn't going be able to sleep until he made sure she was okay.

"Your talents are better utilized elsewhere," the colonel continued. "I'll see what I can come up with for you."

"Elsewhere" meant another sweaty country. Bobby wasn't in the mood.

Besides, he'd been committing too many minor screwups lately. He could only blame his divided mind—he loved Marlie; he lusted after Jane. So far he'd been lucky that no one had died because he was distracted. He couldn't count on that being the case forever.

If one of his men were having the same trouble, he'd insist they take a break, recharge, relax. Get their priorities straight. Which wasn't a bad idea.

"I'm due for a leave, Colonel."

"You always are, yet you never take it."

"I'd like to now, sir."

"Fine. Dismissed."

Bobby hustled himself out of the Pentagon before Delray could change his mind. Then he stood outside trying to figure out where they might have hidden Jane.

The last time he'd had a puzzle like this to unravel had been during the final phase of his operator training for Delta. What was called the culmination exercise.

He'd been brought to Washington, ensconced in a hotel room, then handed a folder with money and instructions for a task—find out how a man had come into the country and if he was still around.

Oh, and while he did this, the FBI was on his tail, with orders to detain, then question him.

Bobby had excelled at that test. He would do no less with this one.

A quick trip to the airport. A short discussion with an airline mechanic, who remembered a limo, a private plane and a very ugly dog, led Bobby to the limo company, and from there it was a short jaunt to the Jefferson Hotel—where he met a brick wall by the name of Serge.

"We do not give out the names of our guests." Serge's French accent was so pronounced, Bobby ground his teeth in annoyance. He'd bet money the man had been raised just south of Cleveland.

"How about this?" Bobby leaned in close and lowered his voice. "I tell you who I think is here, and you tell me if I'm right."

Serge sniffed. "No."

"Tall, blond woman. Ugly one-eyed dog."

Serge was good. He continued to stare at Bobby without a flicker of a single eyelash.

Bobby frowned. Was the man wearing mascara? "Fine."

Bobby strolled toward the bar. She'd have to walk the dog sometime.

Except she didn't.

Had the limo driver lied to him? What purpose

could he have? Maybe the colonel had only pretended to take Jane here, then commandeered another car and taken her somewhere else. It was what Bobby would have done.

He was just about to start questioning the bellmen, when a low *woof,* followed by grumbles, drifted from the kitchen. Bobby pushed through the door. At the sight of him, Lucky began her dance of joy.

The dog walker, a muscle-bound no-neck in an expensive suit, frowned at Bobby, then reached for his weapon. Bobby lifted his hands. "Relax, pal, I'm Luchetti."

"Step away from the dog."

Bobby glanced down. Lucky was licking his leg. He inched out of her reach.

"Where's Dr. Harker?" he asked.

"I don't know who you are," the man said, "but you better back off before I take out your kneecap."

"Luchetti, Captain Robert. I brought the doctor out of Mexico."

The man merely stared at him impassively.

"The dog obviously knows me." Lucky strained at the end of the leash, panting with love. "Just tell Dr. Harker I'm here."

"I don't know who you're talking about. This is my dog. You must have confused the two."

Bobby snorted. "Right. There are so many that look like Lucky."

Lucky woofed once at the sound of her name.

Behind him, the kitchen door opened. Bobby

knew Security was there even before they grabbed his arms and escorted him out of the hotel.

He let them. Standing on the street, he leaned back and stared up, up, up the side of the building.

The only access to that part of the kitchen had been through an elevator positioned in the hall behind some walk-in refrigerators. Bobby had no doubt it went straight to the penthouse.

Which was exactly where he was headed once darkness fell.

CHAPTER TEN

BOBBY HAD TO WAIT UNTIL after 11:00 p.m. before the lights went off upstairs. He didn't intend to rappel down the side of the building, land on the balcony and stroll into someone's cocktail party.

Instead, he planned to rappel down the side of the building, land on the balcony and slip inside the dark, silent penthouse, then discover if Jane was in there. Piece of cake.

No guard on the roof. What *were* they thinking? Of course they hadn't been expecting him.

By 11:20 p.m. Bobby was opening the floor-length patio doors—unlocked, morons—and stepping into the main salon of the suite. Lucky sat directly in front of the doors staring at him as hard as she could with one eye.

"You're more on the ball than anyone else," he whispered.

Her tongue hung out of her mouth when she smiled at him.

"Good girl." Bobby patted her bony head. She slobbered on his hand, and he didn't even mind.

Leaving his gear on the balcony, Bobby went first to one bedroom—empty—then to the second.

The bathroom door stood half open. Light spilled across the carpet and illuminated Jane in the bed. His heart sped up. His throat went thick. Hair unbound and spread over the pillow, she looked like Sleeping Beauty.

"Stay," he whispered to Lucky, then shut the door in her face.

His plan had been to slip in, talk to Jane, tell her what he'd learned. Instead, he found himself slipping across the floor, kneeling by the side of the bed, and then just watching her sleep.

He hadn't thought her pretty, even before the bruises. But now, with the swelling receding and the discoloration fading, she was stunning. Maybe there really was something to the saying that beauty was in the eye of the beholder.

Or perhaps he should fall back on the old standard: absence makes the heart grow fonder. Though his personal favorite had to be…

Only with a kiss will she awaken.

Leaning over, Bobby was a breath away from their first kiss when she slapped him. His ear rang; his cheek stung. But he had the presence of mind to put his palm over Jane's mouth before she screamed.

"It's me," he said urgently.

Her eyes widened, and her lips moved. The sensation shot straight to his groin, and Bobby snatched his hand away.

"What are you doing in here?"

"*Shh!* Do you want them to hear you?"

Her eyes glittered in the half light. "They're here?"

She sat up, and the sheet pooled at her waist. Someone had bought her a very nice negligee. Bobby couldn't tear his eyes from the sight.

He'd thought her flat-chested. He'd been wrong. With the appropriate window dressing her chest was anything but flat.

"How did they get in the country? How did they get in the hotel?"

"Huh?"

"Soldier boy." Jane snapped her fingers in front of his face. "I'm up here."

His face heated. Thankfully the room was too dark for her to see.

"They *who?*" he asked.

She made an exasperated sound. Her chest jiggled enticingly, and he lost his train of thought again.

"You said *they'll* hear. Are there more drug dealers out there?" She tilted her head and a lock of hair fell over one perfect breast. "I don't hear Lucky."

"She's fine. Is that blue?"

He couldn't make out the color of her negligee. Something slinky, silky, blue or maybe purple.

He leaned closer and got a whiff of—"You smell like strawberries."

Jane put one finger under his chin and lifted it until their eyes met. "Did you hit your head?"

"No."

"Who's out there?"

"Lucky. And your guards, I assume. Walking the walk of the terminally stupid."

She laughed, then slapped a hand across her mouth. Bobby found himself smiling, too. Why did he like her so much?

His gaze drifted lower once more. Then again, what wasn't to like?

"Wait a second," Jane said. "Why are you worried about the guards? Did you sneak in?"

"They wouldn't let me see you."

Jane frowned. "They wouldn't let me leave."

"I'm sure your mother and the colonel feel you're safer in here."

"No one is supposed to get in but them. So what's your excuse?"

"What's theirs? It wasn't that hard."

"My mother is going to blow a gasket."

"She should. Anyone could rappel down the building and walk in through the balcony doors."

"Well, hoo-ah," she said quietly. "You did that for me?"

"I didn't drag you out of a hut and through a jungle to let you get killed in your own bed at the Jefferson Hotel."

"But—" Jane's face scrunched in confusion. It was a testament to the healing power of the human body that such an intense expression no longer caused her pain. "The bad guys are in Mexico. Aren't they?"

"If they are, then why the extreme, yet crappy, security?"

"Good question," she murmured. "So what brings you here, Luchetti?"

The word *you* was on the tip of his tongue. But this was about protecting her life, not getting in her pants.

Can't you do both? asked the devil on his shoulder.

"New information," he blurted out before he listened to that devil.

"Spill it."

She shifted and the negligee pulled tightly across her chest. For an instant he thought she might actually pop right out of the plunging neckline. Instead, her leg slid free of the covers—long, strong, tanned. He remembered very vividly having those thighs wrapped around his waist as he—

"Hell."

"Excuse me?"

"Um. What was the question?"

Jane's smile was pure woman. She knew what she was doing to him, and she was enjoying it.

"New information? Bad guys in Mexico? Or no?"

"No. Yes. Hell."

"Again with the hell? Maybe we should just do it first, talk later."

"Do what?"

"Luchetti, you are an idiot. The big it. *Do. It.* You and me."

"Now?"

"It's not like we haven't done it before."

"But that was—"

"An accident? A mistake? A one-night stand?"

"Yes. No. Hell."

"I doubt anyone else is going to break in. We're all alone, except for Lucky. And this bed's much better than the last one."

He'd almost talked himself into the belief that their relationship had been about sex—one night and they were done—but they weren't done.

He'd tried to convince his conscience that what he felt for Jane was lust brought on by having his ego rapped hard by Marlie. He was with Jane because he needed to be with someone, to feel wanted again. But when he looked at her, the explanation didn't wash.

He wanted to be with *her.* Not only was he attracted physically, but he just plain liked the woman. He wanted to be here more than he wanted to be anywhere right now.

Which was such a mind-boggling thought, he wasn't sure what to do.

He should tell her what he'd come to say, then run all the way home to Illinois. But he couldn't. Even before she pulled the straps down her shoulders and shrugged off the lacy negligee.

In Puerto he hadn't taken the time to look. Tonight he did and lost any resistance he might have had.

The garment pooled around her waist, accenting the muscles in her stomach, the rounded weight of her breasts, the pale perfection of her skin. He wanted to run his palm over that skin, his mouth across her belly, press his cheek against her breast. So he did.

She smelled fresh and clean—sun, wind, strawberries. He would never be able to order shortcake again without thinking of her, and maybe that wasn't so bad.

She lay back on the bed and he flipped the quilt to the floor, tugged the negligee down, down, down her legs, to reveal she wore nothing under it.

As she writhed beneath his hands, arched beneath his mouth, clutched his shoulders as his tongue dipped into her navel, he traced lower and lower, teasing, tormenting, making her shatter in his arms.

He collapsed onto the bed at her side. Fingers entwined with hers, he listened as her breathing evened out, then she stirred, raising onto one elbow and staring into his face.

"While I have to admit that was pretty erotic, you need to lose the gun, soldier boy. The clothes, too."

Bobby blinked. He was still dressed, shoulder holster in place. He still had his boots on.

"Sorry." Bobby scrambled off the bed.

"Don't be. I like it that you don't think of anything else but me."

His gaze flicked to hers. For an instant he thought she was making a dig, that she knew about his love for his brother's wife. But her eyes were open and honest. She meant what she said, and he felt like scum. Though he had to admit, when his mouth was on Jane's skin, he *wasn't* thinking of anything else but her.

"The clothes," she reminded him.

He removed his shoulder holster, popped the

magazine, set the gun and ammo aside, then drew his black T-shirt over his head and his black pants over his hips. Seconds later, his boots, socks and underwear followed.

Jane stared at his body, her gaze wandering over him from top to bottom. He shifted, uneasy with her perusal. How had she managed to lie there and allow him do the same without squirming?

Of course, a woman's body was much more beautiful than a man's, and Jane's was the most beautiful he'd ever seen—taut, sculpted by muscle, yet with enough curves to make things interesting. He wanted to touch her all over again.

"Come here," she demanded.

He headed for the bed at a near run.

"Whoa." Jane stood, stopping him with a palm to his chest. "Take a deep breath."

The halting hand turned into a caress as she curled her fingers, skimmed her nails over his nipples, ran a finger down his belly, then followed the path with her lips.

When her mouth closed around him he groaned, and she chuckled, the rumble of the sound skimming along his skin, compounding the nearly unbearable sensation.

Until just recently, he'd had sex regularly. It was amazing, or maybe *not* so amazing, how many women wanted to sleep with a soldier.

However, the encounters had always been hurried, intense, and he'd left as soon as they were over. It was also amazing, or maybe not so amazing, how many women would kill an American soldier for very little money.

But he trusted Jane completely. Enough to relax in her presence and forget about the world for a while. Enough to let her touch him in ways no one else ever had, taking him deeply in her mouth and holding him there for almost too long. Which wasn't very long at all.

He inched her back onto the bed, and when she wrapped her legs around his waist, he thrust inside, gritting his teeth to keep from exploding at the first slick slide of her body against his.

The sensation of skin on skin was one he'd never experienced with anyone else but her. Condoms were a necessity and usually he didn't mind. Better safe than dead. But this was so—

"Good," he said quietly.

"Great." Her voice was hoarse, breathless.

"Spectacular."

"Symphonic."

"Mind altering."

"Mmm."

The desire to kiss her was nearly overwhelming, but her lip was still swollen and bruised. A split appeared to have opened, bled and healed over again. He settled for nuzzling her nose instead.

"Now," she whispered, and tightened around him.

The heat, the friction, the pressure, he couldn't think, he could only feel and do as she commanded, holding her closer.

Now.

JANE WAS ALL TANGLED UP in him—and she wasn't just talking about their bodies. Her thoughts, her emotions, her needs and desires.

Which *so* wasn't good. Bobby had come here for a reason, and it wasn't this. Though she had to say *this* was unbelievable. The man was the best lay she'd ever had.

Jane flinched at her own crude thought. Even seeing it as her subconscious attempt to keep a distance, to not get hurt, she was still ashamed. Sometimes having a medical degree, with the resulting rotation through psychology, was as much a curse as a gift.

She tried to shift away; Bobby pulled her right back.

"Don't," he whispered into her hair.

For an instant she considered pressing the issue, then gave up. She didn't want to leave the circle of his arms. Besides, she'd been the one to suggest the sex in the first place. If he wanted to cuddle, who was she to argue? And wasn't that an amusing gender reversal?

"No condom again," he murmured.

"Still on the pill."

Hey, and this time she wasn't lying, though it hadn't been easy to replace them. Jane had tried to call the pharmacy, only to discover she was unable to access an outside line. She'd had to ask her mother to get the prescription refilled, which had been a lovely conversation. Not.

But at least Raeanne had done what she asked, or

rather seen that it was done. Jane had been una-mused when one of the goons who now lived in the penthouse elevator had laid the package on the hall table.

"I need to get out of here," she said.

"Okay."

Jane pulled back and peered into his face. He stared at her impassively. "Okay?"

"You want out. I'll take you. That's kind of what I do."

She narrowed her eyes. "You came here to tell me something."

Quickly he recounted the information he'd gotten from the man in her village.

"You think my mother is being blackmailed?"

"Yes."

"You don't know my mother. The Senate is her life. She wouldn't do whatever it is they want her to do."

"Exactly. Which is why she sent me to rescue you."

"I have a hard time believing she'd put her career on the line for me."

"I don't."

"Wait until you meet her."

"You keep saying that."

"I keep meaning it."

He tucked her head under his chin, then tossed the cover over them both. "Sleep, Jane. In the morning we'll talk to your mother, tell her what I know, ask what's going on. Together, we'll work everything out."

He sounded so confident; Jane wished she could

be, too. Unfortunately Raeanne Harker was not known for working things out.

She fell asleep easily in Bobby's arms, waking only when he jerked and muttered her name. A quick glance at the clock revealed it was 4:00 a.m.

"Shh," she murmured, and rubbed his back.

He came awake and was immediately alert. His sharp eyes scanned the room even as he reached for the weapon on the night stand.

"Relax." She touched his arm, drawing his gaze back to hers. "No one here but us."

He pulled his hand away from the gun and began fooling with her hair, which seemed to have wrapped around them both.

"Nightmare?" he asked.

"You were the one jerking and mumbling. You said my name."

"I doubt it was a nightmare, then." He waggled his brows.

Jane recognized denial when she saw it. "If you ever want to talk, I'll listen."

"Okay," he said, in a voice that revealed he had no idea what she meant.

"Sometimes talking helps the dreams fade. You give them power by holding them inside."

He sighed. "Jane—"

"You don't have to tell me. Only if you want to. You'd probably sleep better, too. If you didn't see…whatever."

"The problem is, I don't see anything." He took a deep breath and continued. "I don't sleep well because I've trained myself to be hyperalert. Unless of course you and your mutt are creeping out of camp trying to get kidnapped."

Jane blushed. "I said I was sorry about that."

Gently he touched her bruised cheek. "So am I."

"Not your fault."

"Whose was it, then? I was supposed to be protecting you."

"If you want to assign blame, blame the man who hit me."

She could tell he didn't agree. He believed it was his fault she'd been hurt, and she wasn't going to convince him otherwise.

"I asked you about your dreams when we were in Mexico," she reminded him, "and you got all weird."

"Because I don't have any. Or at least any bad ones. And isn't that weird, considering?"

He'd no doubt seen and done some pretty horrible things. Jane had never heard of a person who didn't relive those kind of experiences in their dreams. Such was the nature of the subconscious.

But maybe not for everyone. Just because she'd had one rotation of psychology didn't mean she knew squat about it. That's what psychologists were for.

Bobby moved out of her arms and sat on the side of the bed. "I believe in what I do, and I'm very good at it. Every man I've killed died because he should have."

Once his words would have disturbed her, but not

anymore. Jane had met the Little General. She'd been glad to see him die. She didn't plan to let him invade her dreams, or steal one more moment of her life. Knowing that Bobby felt the same way only made her feel closer to him than when they'd been…what? Making love? This wasn't about love. Intimacy? Maybe. She hadn't truly been intimate with anyone. Ever. But she wanted to try with him.

Tentatively, Jane reached out and touched Bobby's arm. He flinched, but she refused to lift her hand. Instead, she scooted closer and laid her cheek against his shoulder, wrapped her arms around his waist.

"You're the bravest man I've ever met."

She repeated the words he'd once said to her, and he gave a short laugh. In a quick movement, he spun around, pressed her back on the bed and entered her.

The sex was slow and sure, both sweet and sexy. Not another word was spoken, but so much was said.

When it was over and he was sleeping again, Jane stared at the ceiling and wondered why he hadn't kissed her.

She touched her swollen lip. Did he find her ugly? Was this just sex for him?

She remembered the movie *Pretty Woman*. Julia Roberts never kissed the men who paid to sleep with her. A kiss meant so much more than sex.

Could that be Bobby's take, too? Jane didn't know, and she was afraid to ask. She didn't want him to leave and never come back.

As her father had.

She winced as the thought trotted through her brain. She'd sworn never to need a man. She wasn't going to start with this one.

THE WHIRRING SLIDE OF the elevator doors opening into the suite brought Bobby awake. Jane hugged the edge of the bed, as far away from him as she could get.

He frowned. Maybe she just liked to sleep without being all tangled together. Personally, he liked it.

His fingers closed around his gun as he crept toward the bedroom door. Lucky growled—more annoyed than angry. Not a drug dealer, then, but someone she didn't like.

Bobby scooped up his boxers and stepped into them, then he stood behind the door as it slowly opened.

The instant the intruder inched into the room he had his elbow across a windpipe and his gun pressed to a foolish head.

Jane sat up, clutching the sheet to her naked breasts. Her hair was tousled, her cheeks flushed. She glanced toward Bobby and her lips quirked.

"Good morning, Mother," she said.

CHAPTER ELEVEN

BOBBY RELEASED SENATOR Harker as if she had a flaming case of leprosy. "Excuse me, ma'am."

She turned, giving him an icy stare. He snapped to attention. Unfortunately, there was another part of him at attention that could not be disguised by flimsy boxers.

His face heated and the senator's perfectly plucked brows lifted. "And you are?"

"Luchetti, Captain Robert."

"Don't bother to salute," she drawled. "So you're the brightest and the best Delray has to offer? Does the good colonel know you're boffing my daughter."

"Mother, really. Boffing? I'm thirty years old. If you're going to sneak into my bedroom at 7:00 a.m., you're going to see things you weren't meant to see."

Jane got out of bed with the sheet wrapped around her and tossed Bobby his pants. They hit him in the face. He wasn't reacting too quickly this morning. At least not from the waist up.

"When did you get over your aversion to men who carry guns?"

"When other men started pointing them at me with obscene regularity," Jane muttered.

"Hmm." Senator Harker glanced at Bobby. "How did you get past the guards?"

Bobby stood there, uncertain if he should get dressed or continue to pretend he wasn't in his underwear, trying to tame the hard-on of a lifetime in front of the mother of his…

Jane.

"He's Delta Force," Jane answered, and Bobby took the opportunity to set his gun aside and slip into his pants.

The problem was, he couldn't find his shirt. It was probably under the bed. He took a quick glance around the room and stifled a wince. Or maybe hanging from the lamp. He'd have to do without it.

"I'm aware of his affiliation, Jane."

"Then you should know that he can get in wherever he wants, whenever he wants."

"Not exactly," Bobby protested.

"Well, in here, anyway. The guards were a joke."

"Were they?" The senator looked displeased.

The elevator whirred again. Bobby reached for his gun. Senator Harker's eyes narrowed into a contemplative stare.

"Delray?" she called.

"Ma'am," the colonel answered.

Bobby left his weapon on the nightstand.

"Get in here."

Jane made a disgusted sound and stomped into

the bathroom. Bobby stood at attention and waited for his career to go down the toilet.

Colonel Delray stepped into the bedroom; his gaze swept over the well-used bed and settled on Bobby, wearing nothing but his black pants.

"Sir," Bobby said.

"Not you, Luchetti." The colonel shook his head. "Not you."

Bobby wasn't sure what to say. *I couldn't help myself* was probably not the best defense.

He'd been taught to withstand torture, extreme heat, unbelievable cold, boredom, adrenaline—pretty much anything. Yet a week in Jane's company and he'd lost all control of himself. He had no excuse. So he remained right where he was and waited for the worst.

He could always be a farmer. Yippee.

"Luchetti, get dressed and meet me—"

"Just one minute," the senator interrupted.

"I'll take care of this."

She shot the colonel a glare that would have peeled paint off a porch. "According to my daughter, the guards are a joke. This man can get in anywhere he wants to, whenever he wants to."

The colonel shrugged. "No doubt. But I didn't think he'd try to get in here."

"I want him to be her bodyguard."

"Excuse me?" the colonel and Bobby blurted at the same time.

"He's already interested in her body. I'm sure he's going to want to protect it."

"But, Senator, he's Delta Force. He can't operate in this country."

"He isn't going to *operate*. He's going to protect Jane."

"I can't assign an expensively trained man like Luchetti to baby-sit. He's got terrorist cells with his name on them."

Bobby cleared his throat. "Sir, have you asked the senator about what I learned?"

Senator Harker snorted. "There's no conspiracy. No one's blackmailing me with Jane. I wouldn't allow it. But for some reason—probably money—someone is after her." Her gaze sharpened. "You do know I'm a very wealthy woman."

"No, ma'am."

The issue of money had never come up—probably because too many other things had.

"Hmm." She didn't seem to believe him.

"Someone wants her dead," Bobby pointed out. "What does that have to do with your money?"

She didn't answer, just continued to stare at him until Bobby wondered if his fly was open, but he didn't have the guts to look.

"You'd do better to have Luchetti find out who's after your daughter than waste his talents protecting her," Delray said.

"I want the best. According to you, he's it. Make this happen, Delray."

The senator tapped her foot impatiently. The colonel appeared a little ill. Bobby had to wonder why his superior was letting her order him around. Was everything about money?

With the government and the military, sadly, the answer was often yes.

A better question would be, why was the senator behaving so oddly? She wanted Jane protected, yet she didn't seem to want the culprit apprehended, and that just made Bobby's teeth itch.

"I'll do it," he said.

"You can't," Delray began. "You're Delta and—"

"I'm on leave."

The colonel blinked. "That's right. You are."

"If I choose to spend it with Jane…" He spread his hands.

"Not my business." The colonel grinned. Problem solved.

Jane barreled out of the bathroom as if she'd seen a rat, although Bobby had a hard time believing she'd care one way or another about a rodent.

She was dressed in cream slacks and a shirt that was almost pink, but not quite. Her hair was twisted into some fancy knot on the back of her head. Which only made his fingers ache to take it down. The bruises on her face were turning a lovely shade of puce. He barely noticed.

She was an Amazon warrior queen, and she'd come to defend him.

"Don't even think about punishing him, firing him, sending him to Siberia or wherever it is you send people nowadays." She jabbed a finger at the colonel's nose. "If you so much as look at him crosswise, I'll create the biggest media stink you've ever seen. I learned something from you, Mother."

"Relax, Jane. Meet your new bodyguard."

That brought her up short. Her hand lowered; her mouth hung open a little. She turned her gaze to Bobby, and he shrugged.

"Don't you have somewhere to be? Some country that needs butt-kicking, a terrorist who needs killing?"

"Always. But someone else can have the fun this week. I'm on leave."

"You promised me you'd go home and see your family."

"Once you were safe. You aren't safe."

The senator was watching them too closely. Bobby scowled. He didn't want to have this conversation in front of her. He didn't trust the woman.

"I'll get my things and move into the other room."

"Uh-huh." The senator rolled her eyes. "The *other* room."

"Mother," Jane warned. "Put a sock in it."

"I think I have the right to know if the bodyguard plans to continue boffing my daughter."

Bobby plucked his T-shirt off the lamp, shoved his head and his arms through the openings, then settled the dark material over his bare chest.

He could lie to her. But why?

Scooping up his socks and his boots, Bobby met Jane's eyes as he answered her mother, "Yes, ma'am, I do."

He strolled out of the bedroom and into the elevator, Colonel Delray at his side. He felt Delray's censuring glare.

But all he saw was Jane's smile.

"WHAT HAPPENED TO THE woman who didn't want a man?"

"I never said I didn't want a man," Jane pointed out.

"Oh, that's right. You wanted a child and not a husband. Does the captain know?"

"Why should he? We aren't planning on a lifetime commitment."

"You're planning on getting pregnant and sending him on his way?"

"No!"

The absent birth control loomed large in her conscience. But if she hadn't told Bobby about it she certainly didn't plan on telling her mother.

"I have to say, Jane, that getting pregnant by the bodyguard, even if he is Delta Force, would not be helpful."

"Helpful?"

"To my career."

Jane stared at Raeanne. "Mother?"

"Yes?"

"Bite me."

Instead of being insulted and flouncing out of the hotel room, never to return—why should she behave in any way that Jane would expect?—Raeanne merely tapped her pink lips with a matching pink nail. "The Patriot Ball."

"What?"

"The 'welcome back to Washington after a summer of goofing off' ball."

"You never leave Washington," Jane pointed out.

"I won't get ahead if I don't work harder and longer than everyone else."

"Yet some people would consider being a senator ahead enough."

"Not me." Raeanne peered at Jane's face. "The ball's in three days. We'll be able to cover up those bruises by then."

"I am not going to some stupid dance. Have you missed the memo? Someone's trying to kill me. Or maybe kidnap me. I'm still not quite clear on that."

"The security at the Patriot Ball is obscene. Everyone who's anyone will be there."

"Except for me."

"You'll be there."

"No."

"I'll donate a hundred thousand dollars to that shit hole you call a village."

Jane froze, mid denial. "A quarter of a million to the Doctors of Mercy," she countered.

Her mother narrowed her eyes, considered, then gave a sharp nod and held out her hand. Jane hesitated. Why did she feel as if she were making a deal with the devil?

Probably because she was. But for a quarter of a million dollars, she'd not only make the deal but stick to it. Jane put her palm against Raeanne's and gave it a shake.

"Excellent. Now, you'll need a dress."

She stood back, looked Jane over from head to foot and frowned.

Here it comes, Jane thought.

"Have you put on weight?"

"Not since the last time you asked."

"I don't know how we'll find a suitable ball gown at the Big and Tall shop."

"I do not need to shop at Big and Tall. I'm a size fourteen."

Raeanne winced.

"Just because you're a size two doesn't mean fourteen would fit a Holstein. I'm five foot eleven, and my weight is exactly right for my height."

"You know those charts are too generous."

"Those charts are sensible."

Raeanne waved her hand. "Whatever, dear. I'll have some gowns sent over in the larger sizes."

Jane felt the headache begin at the base of her skull. She was gritting her teeth so hard her jaw ached. A common occurrence when she spent more than an hour in her mother's company.

"I'll call the herbalist, too," Raeanne said.

"The what?"

"For your face. We need to fade those bruises."

"Only time can do that."

"You'd be surprised."

Considering her mother was inordinately proud of Jane's medical degree, it always astonished her how often Raeanne turned to alternative medicine. Still, Jane had to admit she'd seen some amazing natural cures during her years in various jungles.

"Fine. Great."

"Then a facial, manicure. Shoes!"

"Mother, for a quarter of a million dollars you can dress me up like Barbie and trot me across the stage like Lassie. But I don't want to hear about it ahead of time."

She could have saved her breath. Raeanne continued to regale her with all that had to be done until Jane's eyes glazed over. Once again, it was Bobby to the rescue.

The elevator door swooshed open and there he was. With coffee.

"Hallelujah," Jane muttered.

Bobby dropped a small knapsack near the door, then crossed the room, doing his best not to trip over Lucky the Prancing Dog. He set the tray on an end table. There were also croissants. She could love this man.

Jane blinked at the thought. She didn't love Bobby. She couldn't. She wouldn't. That was a sure-fire recipe for heartbreak. He wasn't staying. But then neither was she.

"That was fast," her mother said.

"I travel light."

"Hmm." Raeanne eyed his beat-up carryall with obvious disdain. "I need to get a move on if I'm going to make those calls before I have to be on the Hill. Expect the dresses, shoes, et cetera before noon. I'll have the herbalist and the esthetician call before they come."

Bobby opened his mouth and Jane shook her

head. If Raeanne wanted to go, they needed to let her.

Amazingly Bobby kept his lips zipped. Either he was a mind reader, or he wanted her mother gone as much as she did.

He escorted Raeanne to the elevator as if he'd never stood in front of the woman wearing only boxers and the expression of a deer caught in the headlights of a semi-truck.

As soon as the doors slid closed, he turned. "What's up?"

Jane sighed and quickly explained her mother's lunacy. She finished with "Sorry. I know protecting me at a stupid dance is not what you had in mind." She tilted her head. "Actually, what did you have in mind? I'm sure you have better things to do than this."

"Than protecting your life?" His gaze drifted over her battered face, but he didn't seem to notice the bruises. "Not today. Tomorrow or next week, either."

Jane smiled. "You're very sweet."

"*Sweet*. An adjective not often used anywhere near me."

"Nevertheless." Jane poured him a cup of coffee, then filled her own. "Sweet is just what you are."

He snorted.

"We don't have to go to the ball. As my bodyguard—" She faltered over the word and he grinned. "Have you ever been a bodyguard before?"

"Not of so nice a body."

"Right." She shook her head. "You don't have to schmooze me, Luchetti. I'm a sure thing."

"I'm not schmoozing, Jane. You've got the most gorgeous body I've seen in years."

He really seemed to believe that. Of course, he had been hiding in caves and hanging out with bearded men. Which explained a lot.

This was an affair, nothing more or less, and she had to stop herself from slipping into some fantasy land where happily-ever-after was real.

"I have been a bodyguard before," Bobby said. "Usually I protect leaders of small Third World countries who are then deposed or killed the instant we leave said country. They aren't very soft, they don't smell good, and they definitely don't make me happy just to be with them."

"What?" Jane asked, stunned.

How was that for smooth?

Bobby just smiled and took a sip of his coffee. "The ball won't be a problem. Your mother's right. The security there is astronomical. But why is she insisting you go?"

"She's always asking me to attend those things. I always say no."

"You don't like to get dolled up and dance?"

"I'm not a doll and I do not dance."

Bobby contemplated her over the rim of his cup. "Hit a nerve, huh?"

"I looked like a fool in those coming-out dresses."

She shuddered at the memory of the laces and bows, the pastels, which had only made her appear larger and less feminine than she was.

"I'm not even going to discuss the heels. I was

several inches taller than any boy in the room in my stocking feet."

"Poor baby," Bobby murmured. "That must have been tough. Did not one foolish boy ever ask you to dance?"

"I don't know how," she whispered.

"I thought all those fancy schools taught dancing."

They had. Jane just never caught on.

"I know how," Bobby said.

Jane lifted her gaze. "The waltz? Stuff like that?"

"My mother made us learn. Along with lifesaving, CPR and various other basics she thought we should know."

"I like your mother."

"You probably would." He tilted his head. "You want me to teach you?"

"That's okay."

"Until the ball, seems like we've got nothing but time."

He was right, and the thought of swaying to music while being held in his arms was too tempting to resist.

"Sure. Why not?"

Bobby stood, then headed to the entertainment center concealed in a cherry-wood bureau and fiddled with some buttons. Music from the forties slid out—something slow, smooth, sexy. Maybe Glenn Miller. Jane wasn't sure.

Bobby held out his hand. Jane stared at it and hesitated.

"I promise I won't step on your toes," he said.

"But I'm going to step on yours."

He wiggled his foot, covered in a shiny black army boot. "That's the least of my worries."

As if mesmerized, Jane allowed him to tug her to her feet, then into his arms.

She stumbled and would have landed squarely on his toes, but Bobby swung her off the ground, then around and around as if she weighed no more than a child.

The strength of his arms, the press of his body, the whirl of the room made her giddy, and she laughed.

Bobby stopped twirling. Jane glanced into his face and found him staring at her. "What?"

"I like your laugh. You don't do it enough."

Her hair had come loose. A strand stuck to his mouth, and she pulled it away. Her fingertip grazed his lower lip, and his eyes darkened. For an instant she thought he might kiss her. Her fingers clenched his shoulders as something hovered between them— something both old and new, something as ancient and mysterious as the ruins that littered Mexico.

The song ended and silence fell over the room, broken only by the sound of their breath in staccato rhythm. His grip relaxed, and she began to slide down his body. Their mouths got closer and closer, then—

A loud, lively jitterbug tune erupted from the radio, and Lucky, woken from her nap, began to bark. Bobby let Jane go, and instead of descending in an agile, ballet-like movement, Jane's feet hit the ground with an unpleasant thump as he spun away from her to change the station.

"Hush, girl," she murmured, watching his broad back walk away. She blinked as an unpleasant sense of déjà vu, or maybe premonition, wafted over her. He would walk away—it was only a matter of time.

"Never mind," she said. "I'm really no good at this."

"You will be. I promise. You should have seen my brother Dean. Not only left-handed, but two left feet."

"And now he can dance?"

"Kind of."

"What's that supposed to mean?"

"He can, he just chooses not to. Dean's not the dancing type."

"Neither am I."

He returned and pulled her back into his arms despite her protest. "Sure you are. You laugh, you smile, you *will* dance."

Bobby began to show her the steps of a waltz. She tried to follow his feet, listen to his voice explaining what to do, then counting in her ear. But she was too distracted by his touch, his scent, his heat. What was the matter with her?

She'd been bitten by the lust bug. What on earth was she going to do about it?

The same thing she'd been doing. Give in to it.

As she'd told Bobby once before—she wanted this, she wanted him. Since her mother insisted she have a bodyguard, insisted that bodyguard be Bobby Luchetti and insisted they go to the Patriot Ball, Jane was going to enjoy herself while she could.

There'd be plenty of time to live alone without him once he went back to his job.

An hour later Jane was actually getting it. She hadn't tripped in several minutes, nor trod on Bobby's feet for an entire song. He kissed her brow, and she lifted her mouth, begging for more. He didn't notice.

"You're doing great," he said.

"Mmm." She leaned her head against his shoulder, wishing the dance could last forever.

"The colonel thinks you're suffering from a case of rescuer worship."

Jane stiffened. "Excuse me?"

"He didn't want me to see you because he thought you might attach to your rescuer. Sometimes kidnap victims do."

Jane stared into his face as they continued to sway to the music. He seemed bothered by the prospect that she might be sleeping with him because of a misguided sense of gratitude.

He'd asked her that once already, and she'd denied it. She'd deny it again, because she knew the truth.

"I wanted to sleep with you long before the General showed up."

He stilled. "What?"

"A handsome man breaks into my tent and drags me into the jungle. Of course I wanted to jump your bones."

She'd put their relationship right back where it belonged. Now she had to make it stay there.

"You hated me."

"Not for long."

"Because I rescued you." He sighed.

Jane slipped her hands beneath his T-shirt, ran her fingertips over his stomach, then pressed her body against his as the song died.

"If this is rescuer worship," she whispered, "why don't you rescue me again?"

He gazed into her eyes until the next song began, then he took her hand and led her into the bedroom. This time he locked the door.

Then he rescued her. More than once.

THE NEXT FEW DAYS WERE a whirlwind of dresses, shoes, fittings, doctors. Sometimes Jane felt as if she were a princess trapped in the tower. Except her knight was trapped inside, too—as well as a dragon named Lucky.

Or was the dragon named Raeanne? She couldn't decide.

The best part were the nights she and Bobby spent together. Once the army of courtiers and stylists left for the day, they ordered supper, then danced, talked, laughed and retired to the big bedroom for more and more daring games of rescue.

To be honest, Jane wasn't all that enthusiastic about being sprung from the tower. But time moved on, and the Patriot Ball arrived.

The entire day was spent getting ready. Bobby

hung out with Lucky. The two of them would make an appearance in the living room, see Jane with her hair foiled or her nails soaking in warm soapy water, then escape.

One of her mother's flunkies actually tried to help her dress. Jane put a stop to that by throwing out everyone who wasn't Bobby.

As she dressed, all by herself, Jane wondered what would happen when the clock struck midnight and the ball was over.

"Am I Cinderella or Princess Fiona?"

Shaking her head, Jane settled the royal-purple gown over her shoulders. Something had to happen soon. She couldn't live in the tower indefinitely— as much as she might want to.

Jane contemplated herself in the mirror. At first she'd rejected this dress outright, because it was too bright, too attention-getting, too drag-queenish.

But the designer had insisted, "The color is perfect for you."

The woman had been right. This shade of purple made Jane's eyes shine bright green. Of course, the artfully applied eye shadow probably had something to do with it, as well.

"Why does it take an hour to apply makeup so I don't appear to be wearing makeup?"

Lucky, who sat in the doorway watching, merely tilted her head in the opposite direction.

The makeup artist had done an excellent job. Even Jane, who knew exactly what to look for, couldn't see the bruises anymore.

The stylist had swept her hair into some kind of "do," which made it seem as if she wore a crown. The highlights she'd endured turned her tresses from dishwater to gold. The push-up bra gave her cleavage. The gel-crap they'd spread over her chest and shoulders made her skin glow almost as brightly as her mother's diamond necklace and earrings.

"Not bad for Plain Jane of the Yucatán."

"Who called you that?"

Jane shrieked and spun around. Bobby stood in the doorway in a tuxedo. He was so polished, so beautiful, at first she couldn't speak.

Once she could, all she managed was a single word. "Wow."

"Right back atcha."

"I thought you'd wear a uniform." She'd enjoyed some lovely fantasies about taking it off afterward.

"Delta doesn't really have uniforms. We're army, but we're on civilian-clothing status. Besides, the colonel and I felt it best if I blended in."

The reminder that he was coming to the ball to protect her life and not to socialize took a little of the shine off Jane's mood.

Bobby reached out and drew her from the bathroom. "Who called you Plain Jane?"

"Besides my mother?"

Bobby's smile turned into a frown. "She needs her eyes checked."

Among other things, Jane thought, but she kept her mouth shut. She didn't want to spoil this night with discussions of Raeanne Harker.

Lucky pranced around their feet, seeming to know something special was in the air. Jane felt it, too. She was definitely Cinderella, not Fiona. When midnight came she'd still feel like a princess and not an ogre, even if her ball gown turned to rags.

Bobby lifted their hands high and twirled Jane once. The skirt belled out, then settled around her bare legs. She liked the sensation, so she did it again.

She'd balked at wearing panty hose. What good was being a doctor in the jungle if you couldn't go bare-legged?

Jane had taken her nail file to the stockings the dressmaker had sent, and she'd loved every minute she'd spent destroying them.

"Great shoes," Bobby observed.

Jane glanced at the silver sandals—she'd also balked at wearing heels—which had cost almost as much as her dress.

"Italian?" he asked.

Jane lifted her gaze and stared at him curiously. "How do you know that?"

"My sister is a shoe freak. I hear my niece is the same way. Kim was always talking about Rossi this and Fiorangelo that. I guess some of it wiggled into my brain."

He offered his arm. "Shall we?"

Jane hesitated. She'd been excited, now she was just nervous. She'd never attended a dance with a man.

Of course she wasn't "attending" with him. Bobby was her bodyguard.

"Save the last song for me," he whispered.

Their eyes met. All her nervousness fled. As long as Bobby was there, everything would be all right.

CHAPTER TWELVE

BOBBY WAS UNEASY FROM the moment they arrived at the Patriot Ball, and he couldn't figure out why. The security was top-notch, as it should be for such an event. If there was a terrorist attack on this building, or a single nut with a gun, half of Congress and most of the Senate could be wiped out.

He might not have much use for politicians in general, but even Bobby had to admit that if most of them were vaporized, chaos would reign.

He still got shivers whenever he thought about the plane that had gone down in Pennsylvania. If Flight 93 had plowed into the Capitol, 9/11 would have been so much worse. Talk about heroes.

The Connelly Museum was shiny and new, which was why the Patriot Ball was being held there. There was a red carpet of sorts, which the attendees were supposed to stroll across in order to reach the festivities.

Bobby would have preferred to take Jane in the back way, through the kitchen and directly to the ballroom, but her mother insisted they enter through the front of the building like everyone else.

Now he knew why. Reporters and photographers jostled for position behind the security rope. Flash-bulbs popped all over the place.

Obviously the senator was of the opinion that the only purpose to attending such an event was being photographed doing so. Judging from Jane's expression, she couldn't care less. She just wanted this over with.

Men and women wearing dark clothing, with the requisite earpieces, were interspersed though the crowd. If the suits and the ear hardware didn't mark them as Secret Service, their stoic faces and disinterest in anything other than the milling masses would have.

A quick glance upward and Bobby gave a nod of approval. Police snipers on the roof. There was no doubt a fighter jet idling nearby. Nevertheless, that bull's-eye on Bobby's back had started to itch.

"Let's get inside," he murmured.

Great security or not, if someone wanted to take a shot, they could. Which was why protecting a U.S. president was not a job Bobby ever wanted.

They hurried toward the doors. Flashes flashed, questions were thrown their way. They ignored everything as they slipped into the building.

Metal detectors were set up just inside. Bobby showed his documentation, which would allow him to carry a weapon past Security. Amazingly, Jane set off the alarm.

"Metal hip, knee, plate in the head?" the officer asked as she patted Jane down.

"Maybe it's the pins in my hair," Jane suggested.

The woman wanded her and voilà, the apparatus lit up like a switchboard at the *Howard Stern Radio Show*. After probing Jane's coiffure with a pencil, they allowed her to pass.

"That was exciting," Jane said.

"Thrilling," he said dryly. "Do you know how many times that thing's going to ring if hairpins set it off?"

"Do hairpins usually set it off?"

"I don't think so. But how often do people use hairpins these days?"

"You'd be surprised," Jane muttered.

"Jane!"

Senator Harker's voice made them both start. Bobby settled his hand at the base of Jane's spine as they turned to meet her mother. Though he knew he shouldn't keep touching her, he couldn't stop himself. He liked the warmth of her skin beneath the satin, the bump of her body against his.

"Captain." The senator greeted him without looking Bobby in the face.

Jane took another half step closer to him, and Bobby rubbed his thumb over her hip, where no one else could see. She threw him a grateful glance that made him want to turn around and take her back to the hotel for the night.

He didn't understand Jane's relationship with her mother. They didn't seem to like each other at all. They spent little time together, never embraced, and whenever possible they made a jab with words that would have drawn blood if made with fists.

His mother and sister had had their differences, but they'd made up long before his niece was born. Now they were pals, which was disconcerting at times, considering the past, but nice, too.

However, even during the years they'd spent screaming and throwing things, everyone had known they loved each other. Except, perhaps, the two of them. But that was another story. Bobby got the impression the senator and Jane had deeper problems than leftover teenage angst. Especially since Jane was long past the age of majority.

"Jane, I want you to meet my aide, Greg Wylie. He's been working overtime to help organize the ball."

A young man hovered behind the senator. Far enough away that Bobby hadn't even thought they were together, now he stepped forward and extended his hand.

Taller than Bobby, he was slim and blond, with wire-rimmed glasses and the air of the eternally rich.

Jane shook his hand. "Hello, Greg. Mother's mentioned you. You were in the Olympics, right?"

Bobby lifted a brow. Since when did they have an official stick-up-the-ass competition?

"Let's discuss that while we dance." Smooth as a grass snake, Greg tugged Jane into the crowd.

She glanced back at Bobby and he made a shooing motion with one hand. He couldn't very well monopolize her all night. Even if he wanted to.

Bobby took up a position where he could keep an eye on Jane as she whirled by. He'd told her to save the last song, but maybe he should have claimed the first one, too. Seeing her waltz in the arms of another man after he'd been the one to teach her the moves was damn annoying.

The senator sidled up next to him and watched, too. He'd hoped she would find more pressing things to do than talk to him, but no such luck.

"They make a lovely couple, don't you think?"

Bobby grunted. She couldn't be serious. Wylie was a pencil-neck, a paper-pusher, a pasty-faced desk jockey. He couldn't keep up with Jane in a million years. But how to tell that to her mother?

"He's more her type, her class." The senator put a hand on Bobby's arm, and he had to brace himself so he wouldn't jerk away. "I just want you to understand that she might boff the bodyguard, but she isn't going to marry him."

Bobby turned to the senator. "I don't recall asking her."

Senator Harker's smile spread like the Cheshire cat's. "Wonderful. As long as it's a fling for both of you, then no one gets hurt."

"Fling. Right."

Which was what this was. Always had been. There was no reason for Bobby to feel as if he'd been kicked in the gut.

"I have great plans for Jane, and marrying a soldier—even if he is top of the line—isn't in them. She's going to be one of the premier physicians in D.C. before she's forty. Two point five children and a husband on the fast track to the White House."

"Is Jane aware of these plans?"

"Of course. I've discussed them with her on countless occasions."

Bobby couldn't see it. Jane would insist on bringing Lucky. Although the idea of that dog living at 1600 Pennsylvania Avenue was downright amusing.

"Good luck with that," he murmured as he moved off to get a better angle on Jane and Prince Charming.

The night was long. Even longer since he had to watch the woman he'd brought to the ball dance with every other man in the room. Bobby could have claimed a song. He hadn't been forbidden to do so. But she was having such a good time, he didn't have the heart to cut in. Yet.

Jane never forgot him. Every time a song ended she'd glance Bobby's way, even start in his direction. Then she'd be besieged.

She looked beautiful. Of course being a physician and a senator's daughter didn't hurt, either. Especially in this town.

For just one night, she was the belle of the ball. But when the clock struck midnight, she'd go back to being Jane.

And he'd be right there to claim the last dance as his.

JANE HAD NEVER BEEN so popular. Was it the dress, the shoes, her hair? More than likely it was her mother.

After listening to Wylie drone on about his days

as an Olympian, she'd been thrilled to move to the next man.

Then she'd been regaled, more than once, with the news that Senator Harker was certain of a cabinet position within the next few years. Any man in Washington who wanted to ride Raeanne's coattails might consider it worth the trouble to romance her too tall, too smart, not-quite-pretty-enough daughter. Too bad that the daughter only had one man on her mind.

The one who waited patiently at the edge of the dance floor, his blue eyes on her, always, making her remember things they'd done in the darkness and even in the light.

She couldn't wait to get out of here, get out of these clothes, then get him out of his.

"And now, ladies and gentlemen, our last song of the evening."

Jane searched for Bobby, who was already weaving through the throng in her direction. She moved toward him. Someone grabbed her elbow and yanked her back, a little too hard, and she stumbled.

"Doctor, forgive me." Greg Wylie released her. "I just wanted to beg the last dance."

Jane stared at her mother's pet. At one time or another she must have lost her mind and confided to Raeanne the type of man she preferred, because Greg appeared to have been cloned from the description. Yet she had no interest in him at all.

"That would be my dance, Wylie." Bobby had reached her side.

Bobby took Jane's hand just as the other man reached for it. Greg wasn't happy to discover he'd been beaten.

"She can't dance with the help," Wylie sneered. "Buzz off." He took her arm and tugged. Bobby held on to her other hand. Jane felt like a wishbone.

"Hey! You mind?"

She pulled away from both of them. Bobby let her. Greg held on.

Bobby stepped in front of Jane and murmured, "I will break every finger in that hand if it isn't off her arm in one, two—"

Wylie lifted his arms in a gesture of surrender. "Jeez, pal. Relax. A little gung-ho?"

"You have no idea." Bobby twirled Jane away from Wylie toward the center of the dance floor.

His body was stiff; he took a deep breath, let it out slowly, then took another.

"You okay?" she asked.

"Fine. You?"

"Why wouldn't I be?"

"That was unpleasant."

"No. Unpleasant is being at this party when I'd rather be at the hotel with you. *That* was merely annoying."

The tension seeped out of Bobby's shoulders. Jane rubbed her palms over them. "Relax, soldier boy. No one to fight here."

"I like it when you call me that."

"Really? What about when I call you…"

She leaned in and put her lips near his ear.

"Bobby," she whispered breathlessly, as if he were buried deep inside her.

He choked and jerked back. She laughed. He didn't. What was wrong with him?

"I'm sorry you had to stand around all night while I danced."

"That's my job."

"Couldn't have been fun."

"Fun is in the eye of the beholder. I was beholding you. Great time."

She wasn't certain if that was a compliment or sarcasm.

"I'm tired," she said, and laid her head on his shoulder. He was just the right height.

She'd danced all night, with twenty different men, and she'd done fine, because he'd taught her. But she couldn't dance this well with any of them. She didn't *want* to dance with any of them.

"Did you know your mother wants you to get a job in D.C., marry a politician and have two point five children?"

"Uh-huh."

"And what do you say about it?"

"I say that point five child is gonna have it rough."

He let out a burst of laughter, and she leaned back to watch the amusement flow across his face, then settle in his eyes.

The lightheartedness faded slowly, replaced by something darker, stronger, more dangerous. Their steps slowed, and she caught her breath as the whole world fell away.

At last, she thought when his mouth touched hers.

She'd waited for this, longed for it, during every passionate night. She'd begun to think he didn't care for her at all, begun to fear she was nothing more than a brief interlude in Washington. And Mexico.

Maybe that was still true, but at least he'd kissed her. At *last* he'd kissed her.

Bobby's kiss had been worth the wait.

His lips were soft as they feathered over hers. When she responded with a sigh, he delved deeper, tasting her even as she tasted him. His mouth both demanded and claimed.

Perhaps because she'd been injured and was now healed, the embrace was more intense, the kiss an explosion of sensation. She couldn't think beyond the moment, knew nothing but him and her, together at last in a way they'd never been together before.

He tugged her closer, continuing to move them in time with the music. His body hard, his hands firm, yet he held her as if she were a life-size crystal woman, as if she would shatter into a million sharp pieces if he dropped her on the marble floor.

She clutched his shoulders as the music played, and the dancers swirled all around them. In the distance a clock struck midnight.

People had to be watching; her mother would have a stroke: there'd probably be a picture in tomorrow's paper of Jane and Bobby making out. She didn't care.

Bobby lifted his head. Tentatively he touched a finger to her lips. "Did I hurt you?"

She couldn't speak, she could only stare at him mutely as the whole world seemed to shift, even though everything was still the same.

The band stopped playing. Guests started clapping. The clock continued to chime as she and Bobby stood at the center of the universe alone.

Between two chimes there was an odd *pop*. At first Jane thought the clock had broken. But when Bobby's eyes widened and he tackled her, throwing Jane down and covering her body with his, she understood.

It was a good thing she wasn't a crystal woman, because she'd have shattered. If not from being tossed to the ground and leaped on by a couple of hundred pounds of pure muscle, then by the gunshot that had no doubt been aimed at her head.

PANDEMONIUM ENSUED WHEN one of the tuxedoed men fell to the floor, blood flowing from the wound in his shoulder.

Bobby glanced up, gauging the trajectory. He didn't know who that guy was—maybe the shooter had been after *him*—but Bobby didn't think so.

The shooter had been after Jane.

Had to be. If this was a random act or a terrorist plot, the bullets would have kept on coming. There were too many ducks in this pond to stop shooting unless the culprit had been aiming for a certain duck and missed.

Bobby hauled Jane upright and shoved her ahead of him toward the door, putting his body between hers and the gun. Unfortunately, everyone else in the building was headed for the same exit.

"Here."

He grabbed Jane's arm and hustled her down a narrow corridor. In his experience, hallways like this usually led to one place. Finding a door, he opened it just a little and sighed in relief.

"Loading dock."

Which should be secure. The idea of what could be brought in through an unguarded loading dock boggled the mind. Nevertheless, Bobby stuck his head out first. No one shot it off.

No one called out "Halt!" either. He crept outside, telling Jane with a hand signal, to stay behind the door.

The guards lay dead on the pavement.

"This is not good," he muttered.

And he knew in that moment he had to get Jane out of here now.

Quickly he checked the area. As far as he could tell, the sniper had left the roof. Probably went inside at the first shot.

Big mistake. But too late to fix now.

There was only one vehicle—a delivery van that must have been used to bring the caterer's supplies.

Bobby leaped from the loading dock, sprinted to the van and hot-wired the thing in less than a minute. Then he backed it up to the door so Jane could climb inside.

As he spun out of the place, she made her way forward to the passenger seat. "Stay down," he ordered. "Away from the windows."

She sat on the floor. "Someone had a gun."

"Looks that way."

"How?"

"Excellent question."

The only people who should have had a weapon were security forces. So which one of them had taken a bribe from the dark side to put a bullet in the good doctor's head?

"Someone was trying to shoot me, weren't they?"

He glanced at her. She didn't seem shocky or hysterical, so he nodded.

Jane fiddled with a bangle on her silver sandals. Her expression was just a little bit pissed off. *Good.* He'd always found pissed off so much better than scared.

"Now what?" she asked.

Bobby wasn't sure. They could go back to the hotel, which had been secure enough for the past week, but his instincts told him not to. He had to trust those instincts. They were all that had kept him alive on many occasions. He'd have to trust them to keep Jane alive, too.

"I think we should get out of Washington," he ventured.

"Okay."

Bobby turned the van toward the interstate.

"As soon as we get Lucky."

He did a double take. "You can't be serious."

"Can. Am. If I leave her behind, she'll end up in the pound or worse."

"I'll have the colonel take care of her."

"I want my dog."

"But—"

"Arguing is only going to take time. You're some hotshot antiterrorist soldier, aren't you?"

"Counterterrorist," he corrected automatically.

"Whatever. You should be able to sneak in, snatch the dog and be out of there before anyone knows the difference."

She was right, but he tried one more time to change her mind. "Lucky isn't exactly inconspicuous. We're kind of on the run here."

"You plan on stopping for a stroll?"

"No, but Lucky will have to."

"In the woods. Fields. Side roads. Jeez, Luchetti. Who taught you to be invisible?"

The best of the best. Except he'd never had to disappear dragging along a woman in a purple dress and her one-eyed dog.

Bobby turned the van toward the Jefferson Hotel. Moments later, he pulled up at its loading dock.

"Stay out of sight," he said. "If anyone knocks on the doors, don't answer."

"Duh," Jane muttered.

He chose to ignore that and jumped out of the van, locking it behind him.

Just after midnight and the hotel was still busy, though not horribly so. Bobby was continually amazed at how easy it was to walk into a place and not be stopped, as long as he behaved as if he belonged there.

Tonight was no different from any of a hundred

others. He walked in, nodded to a few people and continued to the penthouse, where he grabbed Lucky's leash and Lucky, as well as a few clothes for himself and Jane. He was climbing into the van before anyone knew he'd been there.

Lucky bathed Jane with Lucky love, and the two of them settled on a tablecloth out of sight, while Bobby settled in for a long night's drive.

They'd need to switch vehicles soon. Once the hoopla died down at the museum someone would realize the van was gone. The FBI would think the shooter had it. Then there'd be bulletins, road blocks. He didn't have the time.

"Where are we going?" Jane asked.

There was only one place in the world he could go that, no matter what, he'd be welcome.

"Home," he said. "I'm going home."

CHAPTER THIRTEEN

BOBBY DROVE THROUGH the night. From Washington, D.C., to Gainsville, Illinois, was more than a seven-hundred-and-fifty-mile trip—at least twelve hours.

Once they got out of Dodge, they changed clothes and switched cars—a euphemism for hot-wiring one in a used-car lot, then exchanging license plates in a shopping mall—the colonel would make sure everything was paid for and tidied up later. Jane fell asleep with Lucky's head in her lap, which gave Bobby plenty of time to come to a conclusion.

He no longer trusted Jane's mother.

Deep down, he couldn't make himself believe that Raeanne wanted Jane dead. That was too psycho even for her.

But why had she insisted Jane go to the ball? Why had she hired a bodyguard? If not because she knew something was going to happen there, then because she suspected something was going to happen somewhere, eventually.

Which meant Jane needed to be as far away from the senator as possible until Bobby figured out what was going on.

They should be safe in Gainsville. When a soldier entered Delta Force, he ceased to exist in the regular army. Personnel records were purged from the system and managed from then on by DASR, the Department of the Army Security Roster. Theoretically, no one should be able to find Bobby's permanent address.

Of course, how hard was it to trace a Luchetti in Illinois?

Nevertheless, the family farm was easily defensible. It was in the middle of nowhere, and the land for miles around was flat. No one was going to sneak up on them.

Even if they did, every Luchetti owned a gun, and Bobby was familiar, through a childhood of hide-and-seek, with all the great hiding places on a dairy farm. He couldn't think of a better location to disappear.

They made good time. Bobby used the interstate and stayed just above the speed limit. Too fast or too slow would make a deputy remember them.

He stopped only at very busy gas stations, where he bought coffee, doughnuts and bottled water. Just like every other traveler on the road. He made Jane and Lucky stay in the car. She might think she was plain, but he knew better.

Even without the dress, she was striking. Tall and athletic, she walked with confidence. Her accent was pure East Coast education. And if that wasn't enough—her makeup had started to wear off and it was obvious in the bright sunshine that she was re-

covering from two recent black eyes. In this neighborhood, that could get Bobby's ass kicked by just
about anyone.

He did as Jane suggested, taking detours on side
roads to allow Lucky quick trips into the bushes.
Somewhere in Indiana, while Jane combed out the
snarls in her hair, he called the colonel.

Bracing for a set down, he was pleasantly surprised to hear praise. "Nice job, boy. You saved her
again. And snatched the dog, too. I am impressed."

"What happened to supreme security?"

"No one knows. Everyone's pointing the finger at
the other guy."

"The shooter?"

"Gone."

"How could that be?"

"Why don't you tell me?"

"Loading dock," Bobby said. "Killed the guards.
I must have been right behind him."

The colonel grunted, keeping what they were both
thinking to himself. If Bobby hadn't had Jane to
worry about, he'd have gone after, and no doubt apprehended, the murderer. But Bobby's job was protecting Jane, not chasing killers. At least this week.

"Where are you?" the colonel asked. "The senator is having a conniption."

Bobby wasn't surprised.

"Tell the senator Jane is safe with me."

Bobby hesitated, not comfortable revealing over
any phone where they were headed. Which was why
they had a code for situations like these.

"I'll be where no one knows me," he said.

Translation—where everyone does. Home.

The colonel didn't bother to acknowledge the hint. "Taking the mutt along wasn't bright. Thing stands out like a one-eyed dog in a two-eyed world."

Was the colonel trying to be funny? Bobby didn't think so. Army commanders weren't known for their sense of humor.

"I'll keep that in mind," Bobby said.

"Any news?" Jane asked as he climbed back into the car.

Bobby opened his mouth and she continued, "Besides my mother having a fit."

He shut his mouth and started the engine.

"That's what I figured," she muttered.

They rolled into Gainsville around 3:00 p.m.

"Oh, how cute," Jane exclaimed.

"*Cute* isn't exactly the word I'd pick."

She glanced at him with a frown. "You don't like it here?"

"Mayberry of the Midwest, what's not to like?"

"I can't decide if that means you like it or you don't."

Bobby couldn't, either.

"I haven't been here for…a long time."

"How long's long?"

He couldn't quite recall.

"Years," he said at last.

Jane's eyes widened. "You haven't been home in years?"

"I've been busy."

"So have I, but I go home more often than that. And you've met my mother."

Why *hadn't* he been home? Bobby wasn't quite sure.

He liked his mother, even most of his brothers. Had no problems with his father or his sister. He didn't want to be a farmer, never had. But it wasn't as if he'd be handcuffed to a cow if he ventured into a pasture. He could leave any time that he liked. Unlike Dean, who'd taken over the family business, and by all accounts, was doing very well with it. The farm was all Dean had ever wanted, so there was no reason for Bobby to avoid Gainsville.

Just as he'd avoided calling and telling them he was on his way. They'd welcome him, whenever he showed up, with open arms, but he'd wanted to avert a Luchetti family reunion. He and Jane were supposed to be hiding out.

"The places I've been living lately make your hometown pretty appealing," Jane said.

"I thought you liked it in Mexico."

"I do. But that doesn't mean I don't miss—" Her head whipped around so fast he nearly got smacked in the face with her ponytail. "A bookstore!"

Bobby blinked. Where had that come from? Now that he took a good look, he saw a new hair salon, a family restaurant sporting a family name he'd never heard of, and a great, gray building labeled *Gainsville Memorial,* growing from what he recalled as Mr. Conway's cornfield.

He *had* been gone too long.

"How far is your house?"

Not his. Not anymore—not ever, really. Bobby didn't have a house, which had never struck him as sad before.

"My parents live about five miles out of town. There." Bobby pointed to three silos that rose toward the sky.

"Your father's a patriot?"

"Huh?"

"The flags."

Atop every silo an American flag flapped in the breeze. "Oh. My dad is big on the red, white and blue—was even before I joined the army—but those flags are there because he owns those silos."

"Of course he does. This is his farm."

"Yeah, but, silos cost almost as much as they weigh. It's tradition that when a farmer pays off his debt on one, he tops it with an American flag or paints the icon on the side. A matter of pride, I guess. So everyone who drives by knows how well that farm is doing."

Jane eyed the three towering structures. "They're doing very well, then."

"My dad and my brother are farmer's farmers."

Bobby heard the pride in his voice. Jane must have, too. She shot him an approving glance, before returning her gaze to the horizon.

Moments later Bobby turned onto the winding lane that led from the main road to the stone farmhouse and the bright white outbuildings.

The instant the tires hit gravel, the farm dogs

came running. While most farmers employed canines with herding tendencies such as sheepdogs and collies, or mutts, because they were tough, smart and free, on the farm of John Luchetti purebred Dalmatians ran with the cows, pigs, cats and chickens.

The last time Bobby had been home there'd been only two—Bull and Bear—named for the favorite sports teams of the Luchettis, as well as the majority of Illinois.

However, Bear was a hound, in more ways than one, and his brief affair with a neighboring French poodle had produced doodles. Way too many, judging from the size of the pack.

Bobby stopped the car. Dalmatians and doodles ran around the vehicle as if he'd parked at the center of the Indy 500 track. Bear and Bull jumped in three-foot leaps of joy next to Bobby's window. Lucky pressed her nose to the glass and sighed.

"Wanna play, girl?" Jane asked.

"Is she fixed?"

"There's nothing wrong with her."

"Fixed as in…" Bobby made a cutting motion with his fingers. "Fixed."

"Spayed?" Jane snorted. "Right. In Mexico?"

"Bear has issues."

"I take it Bear is one of those dancing Dalmatians?" At his nod, she continued, "What kind of issues?"

"Can't keep it in his pants. Hence the doodles." He waved at the herd of shaggy, spotted dogs.

"And the other?"

"Bull? He's never shown any interest in girl dogs. We think he's brain damaged."

Jane giggled. The sound turned to a choked garble, and she stared through the windshield wide-eyed.

Concerned the bad guys had beaten them here, Bobby reached beneath the seat for his weapon, even as he followed the direction of her gaze.

His mother stood on the porch.

JANE HAD NEVER MET the mother of anyone she was sleeping with before. She wasn't sure what to do.

Blurting out "He's spectacular" was probably the quickest way to another black eye.

"Bobby? Bobby?"

Mrs. Luchetti bolted off the porch and ran to the car. Dogs leaped out of her way without even being told to move. Either they were all scared to death of her or...

They were all scared to death of her.

She yanked open the driver's-side door. Bobby stepped directly into her embrace.

"Bobby," she whispered.

"I'm sorry, Mom."

"*Shh.*"

She held on to him tightly for several moments. Jane knew she should probably look away, but the pure love, the relief, the sense of family was too fascinating, and too foreign, to resist.

Suddenly Mrs. Luchetti's eyes snapped open, catching Jane mid-stare. She wanted to sit up straight and spill every secret in her head.

"Where've you been?" Mrs. Luchetti asked.

Jane nearly answered, but before she could, Bobby did. "Another assignment. Several, in fact."

"Is she an assignment?"

"*She's* Jane. Dr. Jane Harker. And yes, she is."

Jane fought not to wince. His mother was still staring at her as if she would like to screw off the top of Jane's head and peer inside.

How could he call her an assignment? Then again, what should he call her?

She'd been telling herself not to build any forever-fantasy around Bobby. She didn't want that; neither did he. So his referring to her as an assignment shouldn't hurt.

Shouldn't, but did.

"No one can know she's here for a few days. Okay, Mom?"

Mrs. Luchetti stepped back and put her hands on her ample hips. Her long, white braid swayed. "You came home because you're hiding?"

"Not exactly."

"Let me put it this way, would you have been home today if not for her?"

Jane was starting to flinch every time the woman said *her*.

Bobby glanced from his mother to Jane, then back again. Finally he lifted and lowered his hands, then gave a simple, one-word answer.

"No."

Mrs. Luchetti's sigh was both disappointed and annoyed. Jane braced herself for…what? She wasn't quite sure. Then Lucky squeezed her way through the space between the back and front seat. Jane made a grab, but it was too late.

Lucky hit the ground and was surrounded by spotted dogs. The hair on the back of her neck lifted; she grumbled but she didn't growl.

"What is that?" Bobby's mom asked.

"Jane's dog. We need to keep her away from Bear."

At that moment Bear caught sight of Lucky, yelped and ran for the barn with his tail between his legs.

"Doesn't seem to be a problem," Mrs. Luchetti murmured. "Besides, we got him fixed half a dozen doodles ago."

"I didn't think Dean would ever go for that."

"He didn't have much choice." Mrs. Luchetti reached out and put her hand against Bobby's stubbly jaw. "It's good to see your face."

She tapped him once, lightly, with her fingers, and Jane got the impression that all was forgiven.

The woman leaned into the car. "I apologize for being rude, Doctor. My son hasn't been home in years."

"So I hear."

"And what do you think about that?"

"Mom!"

Jane ignored Bobby and answered. "I think it's criminal."

Bobby stuck his thumbs in his ears and waggled his fingers as he crossed his eyes and stuck out his tongue behind his mother's head.

"Your face is going to stay that way," Mrs. Luchetti snapped.

He immediately stopped as if he'd been spanked. Jane snickered.

"How do you *do* that?" he demanded.

Mrs. Luchetti winked at Jane. "Come on inside, Doctor."

"Jane."

"Jane. I'm Eleanor."

Jane climbed out of the car. Lucky took off with the doodles, leaving Jane to feel as if her toddler had finally started playing well with others.

"What the *hell!*"

A bellow erupted from the rear of the barn. All of the dogs tore back toward the car.

Jane glanced at Bobby and Eleanor. They both muttered, "Dean."

A man came around the side of the building. He didn't walk so much as stomp. Puffs of dust swelled from the ground and swirled across his muck-encrusted work boots.

He was slightly taller than Bobby, leaner, too—more sinew than bulk. His hair was the same shade of dark brown. When he glanced up, Jane was captured by familiar bright blue eyes in a face darkened by a lifetime outdoors. She considered him quite nice-looking, until he opened his mouth.

"Why is there a new dog?" he demanded. "If you can call that a dog."

Jane's lips pursed, and she stepped forward to defend her girl—who appeared to have hidden under the house with the rest of the mutts. No one scared her dog—no one.

She swallowed the words, however, when Dean stopped dead at the sight of Bobby. Joy flitted across his face for just an instant before he scowled.

"About time," he said. "Wondered if you were ever going to be bothered to visit the poor hicks you left behind."

Eleanor shook her head and went inside. Bobby didn't seem insulted. Instead, he strode forward and clapped both hands on Dean's shoulders.

"Damn glad to see you, too."

Dean snorted. But a smile ghosted across his face before he soft-punched Bobby in the gut.

How had such a handsome man gotten such a sour disposition? Wasn't that always the way? Either that or all the good ones were gay.

"Have you talked to Colin?" Dean asked.

Bobby dropped his arms. Tension radiated from him. He turned sideways, away from Dean, but Jane still couldn't see his expression.

"This is Jane," he said.

Dean glanced at her, then back at Bobby. His knowing look made her want to kick him in the shin. Childish, but then so was he.

"Aha."

"Shut up," Bobby said. "She's going to stay for a few days."

"And you?"

"I'm going to stay, too."

"Aren't we the lucky ones?"

Bobby ignored him, which Jane was starting to understand was the preferred method of dealing with this crabby family member.

"You think you can keep your trap shut, and everyone else's too?" Bobby asked. "We need to lie low."

Dean's gaze flicked back to Jane again. "Trouble?"

"Times ten."

"Then consider my lip, and everyone else's in the vicinity, zipped."

"Daddy!"

A boy of about six or seven barreled out of the barn. With bright blue eyes, freckles and untamed light brown hair, he brought to mind Tom Sawyer, an image heightened by his stained overalls and torn shirt. He tripped over his huge feet and landed in a heap in front of Dean.

The man reached down and hoisted the kid upright. "You okay, Tim?"

The hand he ran over the child's messy hair was big and rough, but the touch was gentle, as were the words.

Tim stared up at Dean with such utter trust and love, Jane gave the man a second look. In his eyes she saw the same expression, and her initial dislike fled. No one could be that bad if they loved a child that much.

Every doodle scrambled out from under the porch and tried to knock Tim down again. Lucky came out, too, and joined the fun.

"Who's the new one?" Tim asked between giggles.

"Don't get attached, kid. It's only here for a few days."

It? Jane's annoyance returned.

"But she's so sweet!"

The little boy had gone down on his knees and was busy getting Lucky love all over his face. Jane winced, but Dean didn't seem to care. The child no doubt wallowed in a lot worse things than dog spit.

"Who's that guy?" Tim shut one eye and squinted with the other. "He looks kinda like you."

"Except I'm more handsome." Bobby punched Dean in the arm.

"Ow! Watch it, G.I. Joe. Some of us aren't muscle heads."

"G.I. Joe!" Tim leaped to his feet and threw his arms around Bobby's knees. "You're Uncle Bobby! We thought you was dead. At least twice. Gramma cried."

A flicker of sadness passed over Bobby's face.

"Tim," Dean warned.

"She did. And Grampa said, 'Ellie, he'll come back.' And here you are. Grampa's always right."

"Or so he says," Dean muttered.

Tim lifted his arms in the air. "Pick me up."

"You're kind of big for that, aren't you?" Bobby asked.

"You're huge. Can't you do it?"

"Sure." He lifted Tim into his arms, then tossed him toward the sky.

"Hey!" Jane exclaimed. "That can't be safe."

"With Tim," Dean said dryly, "that's about as safe as he gets."

Lucky danced around their feet, barking. When the doodles began to chase one another's tails, and things started to get really out of hand, Jane whistled.

Obediently, Lucky trotted out of the fray. Bobby set Tim down, and the boy followed the dog, albeit erratically. Way too much tossing for one little brain.

"Hi."

He peered up at her, showing off adorable gaps where a few teeth should be. Jane was suddenly possessed by the urge to produce five or six just like him.

"I'm Tim Luchetti. I used to be The Timinator, 'cept Dean, that's my daddy, said I needed a shorter first name and a better last one. Since I didn't have a last one and my name used to be Rat, before it was Timinator, that wasn't too hard."

He spoke as fast as he walked, and he danced around as if he had to pee during the entire conversation. Jane suddenly understood what Dean meant when he said flying through the air with Bobby was safe in comparison. She had a sneaking suspicion Tim had attention deficit hyperactivity disorder— ADHD—and her assessment of Dean rose another notch.

"I'm Jane." She held out her hand.

"Dr. Harker," Dean interjected.

"Jane's fine."

"How 'bout you be Dr. Jane," Tim said. "I like that."

His hand slipped into hers. Instead of shaking it, he held on tight and dragged her toward the house.

"Come and see my football. It's soft, 'cause Gramma says I throw too hard. Do you like football?"

Jane glanced over her shoulder at the brothers, but they had their heads together in what appeared to be a deep and serious conversation.

"Sure." She turned to Tim. "I like football."

He squinted at her from beneath bangs that were half an inch too long. "Can you catch? My aunt Kim said she could, but she can't. The ball hit her in the nose, and that's how I ended up with the soft one. Did you get hit in the nose?"

Jane remembered her fading bruises. No one else had mentioned them. Probably because bruises around here were as plentiful as…cows.

"Not exactly," she said, unwilling to explain drug dealers, kidnapping and murder to a child.

"Someone smacked you around," he said sagely. "That used to happen to me a lot."

Jane frowned. "Where?"

"I can't remember. Before here. No one *ever* hits me here."

"I would think not!"

Tim contemplated her with a far-too-serious expression for a child of his years. "Next time anyone tries to smack you, you gotta get small, hide, duck. Then find someone who'll protect you."

Jane glanced at Bobby again. He saw her looking and smiled.

"I did," she whispered, then followed Tim into the house.

CHAPTER FOURTEEN

"WHAT'S WITH THE DOCTOR and the longing looks?" Dean asked.

Bobby started. He'd been staring after Jane, remembering the last time they'd—

"Huh?" he asked.

"Man, for the smartest one of us all, you sure are dumb."

"I'm not the smartest. That's Kim."

"The princess lawyer. She is *so* annoying."

Dean and Kim had always been at odds. However, when Dean's best friend had gotten Kim pregnant not once, but twice—albeit fourteen years apart—Dean had beaten the crap out of Brian Riley. Some things were a matter of principle.

Since then, Kim and Dean had called a truce of sorts. Although, Bobby doubted they'd ever be able to quit ripping on each other at every opportunity. Habits born in the cradle died hard.

"I'm sure it'll be handy to have a lawyer in the family," Bobby said.

"I guess."

They'd have to use a cattle prod to get Dean to admit needing Kim for anything.

"You gonna add a doctor to the mix?"

"Huh?"

The word seemed to be Bobby's sole response to a lot of questions lately.

"The *doctor*. Is she gonna be Mrs. Luchetti number…" Dean counted on his fingers. "Five?"

"No." Bobby frowned. "I went to Quintana Roo to rescue her, then we escaped and then— Well, it's complicated."

"Don't tell me you aren't sleeping with her. I'm not that stupid."

Bobby kept silent. He wasn't going to comment. Especially to Dean.

"Are you still in love with Marlie?"

Bobby flinched. "How can I be? She's Colin's wife. She's already on kid number two."

"That doesn't mean you can't love her," Dean said quietly.

"I barely knew her."

And the more time he spent in Jane's company, the more time he spent in her bed, the less and less he thought about the woman he'd once planned to marry. But was that good or bad?

"Mom's worried."

"I'm home now."

"She's worried that you and Colin having this fight over a woman is going to break up the family."

"There wasn't any fight."

"You punched him in the mouth."

Bobby made a derisive sound. "That wasn't a fight, that was…"

"Fun?" Dean suggested.

Bobby shrugged. Punching Colin hadn't made him feel any better.

"Tattletale," he muttered.

"Colin didn't tell. Marlie did."

Bobby winced again. She had to think he was a beast, coming to their house and smacking her husband in the mouth.

"That's over now," he said.

"Mom thinks you'll run back to some foreign country where you'll disappear for another few years."

Dean stepped closer and gave Bobby a shoulder in the chest. Bobby took a step back. "And if you do that to her, I will personally dig through the sand of a whole shitty country to kick your ass."

"I thought you were giving up swearing."

"I'm trying." Dean got out of Bobby's face. "It's a lot harder than I thought."

The porch door slammed, and they both turned to discover their father striding across the yard.

John Luchetti appeared well. Though he'd had a heart attack a few years ago and been forced to cut back on the farm work he loved, as well as red meat, beer and cigarettes, he'd found other things to do. Like traveling with his wife, taking care of his grandchildren and sneaking red meat, beer and cigarettes.

John pulled Bobby into his arms. "About time, son," he whispered, then he just held on.

Throughout childhood their father had been the voice of reason in a house of insanity. Bobby couldn't blame his mother for being on edge. Too many kids, too close together, did that to a woman. Make five of them boys and they were lucky she wasn't in a corner talking to her toes most of the time. Not that she hadn't, mind you, but she usually stopped after a few hours.

Dad had been the calm one, the sane one, the one, despite their mother's daily fury, that you *did not* screw with. When the man spoke, they all listened. Except for Dean. For some reason John and Dean struck sparks off each other to this day.

"Everything good?"

John released Bobby, then smacked him on the shoulder in lieu of a kiss. Luchetti men might hug, but they drew the line at kissing.

"Good enough," Bobby answered.

"Met the girl." John patted the pocket of his work shirt in an eternal hunt for the pack of cigarettes that was no longer there. He glanced hopefully at Dean.

"I quit," Dean murmured. "Mom's got a nose like a bloodhound."

"Can't think it would hurt to have one cigarette a day. But *no*." John lifted his chin in Bobby's direction. "So tell me about the doctor."

Quickly Bobby explained about Mexico, D.C., drug dealers, kidnappers and snipers, which took less time than he would have thought.

"You think we can keep things quiet for a few days?" Bobby asked.

"Maybe," John said slowly, thoughtfully. "We don't have to go to town, but you know how people love to visit. We'll keep an eye on the road. Anyone shows up, you two get out of sight."

"My plan exactly."

"Tim's got eyes like a hawk, and he knows everyone's vehicle. Strange car coming down that road, he'll ring the dinner bell."

Since Bobby couldn't buy better security than a six-year-old with a dinner bell, he nodded.

His dad clapped him on the back, the force of the blow indicating the level of his joy at Bobby's homecoming. "Your old room is exactly where you left it, son."

JANE WAS PLAYING CATCH with Tim when a car turned into the lane. Tim glanced that way, then continued throwing the football, so Jane assumed the vehicle was one he knew.

Bobby, Dean and John had gone into the barn to examine a new bull. Jane had declined. She'd seen quite enough bull in her life, thank you.

Eleanor was cooking supper. She hadn't wanted any help. Since Jane was lousy at cooking, but not too bad at playing with little boys, she didn't mind.

Lucky kept trying to steal the ball and give it to the doodles. They'd finally locked all the dogs behind a fence, where they ran back and forth barking until Eleanor shouted, "Knock it off!" from the kitchen window.

Only Lucky was dumb enough to bark one last

time. The sound ended on a yelp when one of the others snapped at her tail.

The car rolled to a stop just as Bobby appeared in the barn doorway. A woman got out of the passenger seat; her gaze went directly to him and she sprinted across the yard, launching herself into his arms and planting a big smooch right on his lips.

"That had *better* be his sister," Jane muttered.

"She's Kim. Sister. Yep."

Tim fired the ball right at Jane's stomach.

"Oof," she said, and doubled over.

"Hey, you okay?"

Bobby was already on his way over. She waved him off. "I'll live."

He took the football from her hand, then threw it over the fence. One of the doodles grabbed the thing and was gone.

"Fetch, kid," Bobby said, and Tim scampered off.

Bobby's sister studied Jane as if she were a slide under a microscope. Jane stared back with the same expression. One girl in a family of six. Jane, an only child, couldn't imagine what that had been like.

Kim Luchetti, now Riley, was tiny. Even with the two-inch heels, which were completely inappropriate for the gravel driveway, she came in at just over five feet tall. She was pretty and petite. Something Jane would never be, and she wanted Kim to like her so badly, she could barely breathe.

Bobby introduced them. They shook hands. Smiled. Nodded. Then a whirlwind in a hot-pink dress erupted from the car.

"Mommy!"

The little girl with bright green eyes to match her mother's and curly light brown hair to match that of the man chasing her ran straight past Kim and threw herself at Jane.

"Up!" she shouted.

The child's shoes matched her dress, as did the ribbon in her hair.

"Okay, that's just cute." Jane picked her up. "You've got to be Zsa-Zsa."

The child grinned and threw her arms around Jane's neck for a hug.

Jane glanced over Zsa-Zsa's head. Kim stared at her with a contemplative expression.

"Kids like me," Jane explained.

"Kids are usually right." Kim walked past her and into the house.

Jane wasn't sure, but she thought that might be a compliment.

"I'm Brian." Jane glanced at the girl's dad. "I'll take her."

"Noooo!" Zsa-Zsa's arms tightened, nearly choking Jane.

"I guess no," Jane managed, and Zsa-Zsa loosened her hold. "She's fine. Really."

Jane had always liked the feeling of a little body clinging to hers like a monkey. For a change, the child she held wasn't feverish, dying or abandoned. Life was good.

Unless she decided to dwell on the fact that someone was trying to kill her.

"Supper!" Eleanor shouted.

People converged on the house from every direction. Dean released Bull and Bear from the pen at the side of the barn. They charged up the lane.

"If a car comes down the road," Bobby said, "they'll lose what's left of their minds."

A Midwestern farmer's answer to electronic surveillance.

Supper consisted of chicken, potatoes and vegetables, and lots of it. The conversation revolved around the Luchetti and Riley farms, Kim's last year of law school, which she would begin in the fall, and Tim's progress with his meds.

Jane had been right; the boy suffered from ADHD. What she hadn't figured was that Dean had been diagnosed with the same thing. No wonder the two had bonded.

"Tell us about your work, Jane," Kim said.

Jane had been enjoying the flow of conversation all around her while she tried to keep Zsa-Zsa from spreading mashed potatoes through her hair. When everyone turned their attention toward her, she stuttered, "I—uh—"

"Jane's a physician with the Doctors of Mercy," Bobby said. "She provides medical care to disadvantaged countries."

"Can't be much money in that," Dean observed.

"Hardly any."

"I thought most folks became doctors to get rich."

"And here I thought they did it to help sick people."

Kim giggled. The sound made Zsa-Zsa laugh and clap her hands together. The resulting shower of mashed potatoes, in which her chubby little fingers had been covered, speckled Jane from forehead to neck.

Zsa-Zsa's eyes went wide; her mouth made an *O*. The entire family stared at Jane, waiting to see what she'd do. Was this a test? How did one pass? Worse, what if she failed?

Jane couldn't help herself as she took in the expression on the little girl's face, the mashed potatoes dripping off her own nose... She snickered, choked, and then she couldn't stop laughing.

BOBBY HAD NEVER HEARD Jane laugh like that. Oh, she'd laughed, and he'd been charmed. But he'd never heard her snort, giggle and guffaw. He was more than charmed; he was turned on.

So when she excused herself to wash up, Bobby waited only a minute before he did the same. Nobody even noticed. They were too busy cleaning off Zsa-Zsa, the floor, the wall, and chattering as they talked louder and louder in an attempt to hear one another. Even though so much had changed since Bobby had left, he still felt as if he'd never even gone.

He climbed the steps to the second floor, which sported three bedrooms and one bath. The halls seemed to ring with the ghosts of the arguments that had ensued over that single bathroom, since Kim had hogged it more than if they'd had three sisters instead of one.

Their parents' room had been moved to the attic, beneath the eaves, at about child number four. They had their own bathroom. No one could ever accuse the elder Luchettis of being slow on the uptake.

Bobby glanced into his and Colin's old quarters. His dad was right. Everything appeared pretty much the same.

He could still see the line they'd drawn in Magic Marker down the center, could hear their childhood voices vowing to stay on their own side. That had worked pretty well until their mom walked in.

They'd spent the following Friday night repainting the wall and all day Saturday scrubbing the floor. They'd never completely erased that line, and their mother had never let them forget it.

But no matter how much he and Colin fought, no matter what they'd said or done to each other during the day, when the lights were off and they lay in their bunk beds, they'd talked about everything—girls and school, dreams and hopes, secrets and fears.

A sense of nostalgia, of loss, filled Bobby. Would he and his brother ever retrieve the closeness they'd once shared?

"I guess I know which side of the room was yours," Jane said from behind him.

"Not much of a mystery."

While Colin's half was papered with pictures of faraway destinations torn from magazines and newspapers, Bobby's had toy soldiers marching across the shelves attached to the wall and a camouflage shade on his desk lamp. He wasn't even going to mention the khaki sheets on his level of the bunk bed.

Jane leaned over Bobby's shoulder to get a better look. Her breasts pressed into his back. He remembered the sound of her laughter and the flavor of their very first kiss.

Spinning around, he took her in his arms, swallowing her surprised gasp, tasting mint on her tongue. She'd not only been cleaning mashed potatoes off her face but brushing her teeth.

"Mmm," he murmured, and relished the feel of her lips beneath his.

Her hair had come loose from the fancy crown of the night before sometime between D.C. and Ohio. She'd tossed the pins out the window and let the breeze stream through her hair.

The memory reminded him of what he'd felt like then—uncomfortably hard and unable to ease the tension between his legs since they'd been busy running for their lives.

However, they were safe now, and there was a bed too close to be ignored.

That they'd never kissed before last night, though they'd slept together many times, had made the embrace unbelievably erotic. Even on the dance floor, in the middle of hundreds of people, he'd been so aroused, the only thing that would have kept him from sneaking into a linen closet and taking her against a wall was a near-death experience.

Bobby started to back slowly into his old room,

pulling Jane with him. As enraptured with the embrace as he was, she didn't realize what Bobby was up to until he pulled her onto the lower bunk along with him.

"Hey! What's the deal?"

"I always wanted a woman in my room."

She smiled. "Childhood fantasies?"

"Adolescent. You wanna make my every dream come true?"

"If it involves having sex while your entire family eats supper one floor below, I'd say, no."

He pushed her back on the pillow, then rolled on top of her. "How about we just make out?"

"Okay."

She wrapped her arms around his neck and her ankles around his calves. The resulting shift in position dumped his lower body onto the mattress right between her thighs. He could get used to this.

Her tongue slid along his lower lip, then her teeth tugged just a little. She tightened her hold, pressing her breasts against his chest. He wanted to tear off her clothes, bury himself inside her and stay there for a week and a half.

He'd never been this hot for a woman. Maybe he should try abstaining from first base more often.

The sex had been great in Mexico, even better in D.C. In Illinois, he had a sneaking suspicion it would be spectacular.

Bobby forgot they were only supposed to be making out. His hand crept under her shirt, slid along her ribs, sidled across the slight fullness of one breast and settled over the peak. She rubbed herself against his palm as he rolled the nipple with his thumb.

He remembered taking her in his mouth in the darkness, the taste of sweet flesh on his tongue, the softness of her skin against his chin, the sensation of a nipple against the roof of his mouth as he suckled her until she cried out over and over and over again.

She reached between them, cupping him through his jeans, and he nearly lost control for the first time since he was fifteen.

He went still, then lifted his mouth and rested his forehead against hers. "Sorry."

"For what?"

Her voice was breathless, as if she'd just run ten miles, or been rolling around with him on a bunk bed trying to make him come.

"We weren't supposed to be doing this."

"Why not?"

Her eyes were heavy, her lips wet and full. He still had his hand up her shirt, her nipple between his thumb and forefinger. He couldn't stop himself from caressing her. She was both soft and hard, a tantalizing combination of contrasts.

He tried to remember why not, too. "Door's open."

"Is there a lock?"

"No."

His parents had a lock on *their* door. They'd taken a lot of "naps" when he was a kid. But locks weren't allowed on any other doors. As his mother had always said whenever anyone asked: *Got something to hide?*

"We should—"

Jane flexed her fingers, nails scraping the hardened length of him. He drew in a sharp, hissing breath and forgot what he'd been about to say.

He had to count backward from twenty, trying to get his mind off the heat, the need, the throbbing in his brain, his pulse, his groin. It wasn't working.

The only thing that could cool him down faster than a bullet whistling past his head was his mother's voice from the doorway.

"This doesn't look like an assignment to me."

CHAPTER FIFTEEN

JANE HAD THOUGHT THE phrase "my blood froze" just an expression, but she learned differently with a jolt like an ice-cream headache right between the eyes.

She shoved Bobby. Since he was in the act of scrambling off the bed, he fell on the floor. She thought she heard choked laughter from his mother, but when she glanced at the woman's face, there wasn't a hint of amusement to be found.

Jane sat up, searching frantically for a bright side to this fiasco. At least Eleanor had gotten here before they'd torn off each other's clothes.

"Jeez, Mom. You mind?"

"Actually, I do." Eleanor's blue eyes, so much like her son's, met Jane's. "In this house, there's no sleeping together without a marriage license."

Bobby made a disgusted sound. "I'm thirty-three."

"Congratulations. You still don't get to do her under my roof."

Bobby winced. "Mom!"

"Just once I'd like a Luchetti grandchild to arrive more than nine months after the wedding."

"We aren't—" Jane began.

"Looked like you were just about to."

"Getting married," Jane finished.

Eleanor tapped her foot on the wood floor. "Then you—" she jabbed a finger at Bobby "—sleep at Dean's house."

Without another word she spun on her heel and marched out. When she reached the ground floor she shouted, "Hey! Supper's downstairs."

Jane cringed. So did Bobby.

"Sorry," they both said at the same time.

"You think she'll tell the family?"

"I don't think she'll have to."

Jane's headache got worse, and she put her fingertips to her forehead as she groaned.

"Why don't you stay here." Bobby was still on the floor. He scooted closer and laid his hand on her knee. "Lie down. Rest. You've had a rough…"

"Month?"

"Near enough."

"That's too cowardly, even for me."

"Cowardly? That's a word I'd never put in the same sentence with you."

"Thanks." Jane got to her feet. Bobby followed. "Come on. Let's face the music."

Bobby glanced down. His pants still appeared to have a sock stuffed down the front. "I need to use the bathroom," he muttered, and fled.

Jane decided not to wait. She'd faced more frightening things than Bobby Luchetti's mother. She wasn't going to start hiding now.

Downstairs, she went straight into the dining room, meeting everyone's gazes head on.

Brian, Zsa-Zsa and John barely glanced up from their plates. Dean smirked. Big shock. She stuck her tongue out when his mother wasn't looking.

Except Eleanor zeroed in on her so suddenly, Jane was left with her tongue curled toward her nose and her face twisted. Eleanor merely lifted a brow. Kim grinned and gave her the thumbs-up.

"Where were you and Uncle Bobby?" Tim asked. "Daddy thought he was getting in your pants."

Bobby barreled into the room at that moment and stopped dead just inside the door.

"But he's still in his own pants. Daddy, how could Uncle Bobby be gettin' in Dr. Jane's pants? He's way too big for 'em."

Jane's face flooded with heat. She wanted to crawl under the table, or maybe beneath the porch with the doodles.

"Nice." Thankfully, Eleanor was staring at Dean and not at Jane. "I leave the room for one minute and you're teaching him a new expression. Keep it up and the judge is not going to agree that Tim's better off with you than anyone else on the planet."

Panic filled Dean's eyes. Tim started bouncing in his seat. "Whad I say?" he asked.

Dean put a hand on the boy's shoulder and Tim immediately stopped bouncing. "Never mind, kid. Go feed the dogs."

Tim leaped off the chair. "'Kay!"

The room went silent. Eleanor cleared her throat.

"I apologize," Dean said. "My mouth gets away from me."

Jane considered the man. Knowing that he had ADHD, like Tim, explained a lot. The impulsiveness that marked the disorder was often evident in an inability to keep quiet.

"Forget it," she said.

The room seemed to breathe a collective sigh of relief.

"Especially since he was right," Bobby muttered as he took a seat next to her.

Jane glanced at the others, but no one appeared to have heard, or if they had, they'd chosen to ignore him. She kicked Bobby under the table.

Her gaze met Kim's. Bobby's sister's eyes were full of both speculation and amusement. "Why don't you come on over to my place tomorrow," she said. "You're going to be bored sitting around here. Lord knows, I was."

"Yeah, but you were the Princess Lazy," Dean said.

"Was not."

"Was *not!*" Zsa-Zsa shouted.

Brian scooped his daughter out of the high chair. "Now you did it."

He carried her out of the house as she continued to chant, "Not, not, not, not, *not!*"

"I hate to say it—" Kim stood "—but she's exactly like her mother. We'd better go."

Shouts of "Doodies!" "Timmy!" "Kitties!" followed, then the car started and all was silent again.

Eleanor began to clear the table and Jane did, too. "You're a guest," Eleanor said. "Sit."

"I'm more of an intruder. The least I can do is KP."

Eleanor shrugged, then shooed the men outside to put away the dogs.

"If you leave those darn doodles loose they bark all night. Besides—" Eleanor led the way into the kitchen "—we should talk."

Jane bobbled the stack of plates, but recovered before they fell on the floor. "Talk?" she echoed.

"About you and my son."

"Do we have to?"

Eleanor just glanced at Jane, then turned on the dishwater, filling the sink.

"Obviously you're more than an assignment."

"Not according to your son."

"He's never brought a girl here before."

For some reason, the knowledge perked Jane right up. Nevertheless…

"I'm not exactly a girl, and he didn't have much choice."

"One thing about Bobby, no one pushes him around. If he didn't want to bring you, he wouldn't have."

"Maybe."

"You're thinking it's a fling."

Jane didn't bother to answer. This was Bobby's *mother*. She was not going to discuss "fling" or "not a fling" with Eleanor Luchetti.

However, Eleanor wasn't going to be dissuaded

by anything as simple as silence. "But I'm thinking you could turn this into a whole lot more if you put your mind to it."

Jane dropped a fork on the floor, narrowly missing her toe. "What are you saying?"

"Seduce my son."

"Again?"

The word escaped before Jane could snatch it back. Eleanor merely smiled. "Whatever it takes to—"

"To what?"

"Keep him here."

"Here?"

"Well, not *here,* exactly. In the country." Eleanor's shoulders slumped, and she stared at the fading suds in the sink. "I don't think I can take having him disappear again."

Jane realized her mouth was open. "You want me to—"

"Do whatever you have to do to make Bobby quit his job. Marry him. Have his baby. Have ten. He won't leave if he has responsibilities here."

Jane wasn't sure what to say except "I can't."

"You can sleep with him, but you can't love him? You can let him save you, but you won't save him?"

"He's good, really good, at what he does. I couldn't take that away from him, and I couldn't take him away from the world. Without Bobby I would have died, and so would a lot of other people."

"If he keeps doing what he's doing, *he's* going to die."

"I don't think he will, not anytime soon."

Eleanor turned her head. "You love him, don't you?"

"What?" Jane yelped.

She'd refused to give a name to the feelings she had for Bobby beyond lust. If she didn't admit to anything more she couldn't get hurt. Or so she kept telling herself.

"Only someone who loved Bobby would understand that being a soldier is part of who he is. Take that away, and he'd be miserable."

Jane contemplated Bobby's mother for several ticks of the clock. "You don't want him to quit."

"I do, but I understand that he won't. He can't."

Jane had a fleeting wish that her mother understood her as well as Bobby's understood him. Raeanne would forever be trying to get Jane to become the doctor of the elite. She'd never comprehend that to take away Jane's work with the Doctors of Mercy would be to take away a part of her soul.

"So you were playing me," Jane said.

Eleanor cast her a quick, uneasy glance and Jane smiled. "I've got to admire that."

BOBBY HOVERED OUTSIDE the kitchen door. He'd planned to help Jane and his mom with the cleanup since his dad, Tim and Dean appeared to have doodle herding down to a science.

He'd stopped when he heard his name, then he'd been unable to leave once he realized what they were discussing. He'd known Eleanor was testing Jane long before Jane figured it out. He should have stepped in then, but when his mother had said Jane loved him, he'd been frozen, unable to interrupt, too interested in what Jane would say.

While she hadn't really answered the question, she hadn't denied loving him, either, and that had made Bobby think as he wandered out of the house and across the cornfield to the thresher's cottage, then took a seat on the front porch.

Could a woman like Jane and a man like him…?

"Nah," he muttered.

"Talking to yourself?" Dean stood on the other side of the screen door.

"I thought you were chasing doodles."

"Done. I just put Tim to bed." Dean contemplated Bobby for a few seconds. "Want company?"

In the past, a conversation with Dean had produced the same headache Bobby got when someone threw him into a wall. But his brother seemed older, wiser and, amazingly, less sarcastic than the last time Bobby had seen him. Age, responsibility, the love of a child had matured him—or at least calmed him down.

"Sure," he found himself saying.

Dean stepped through the door and took a seat, as well. "What's up?"

Bobby hesitated. If Colin were here, Bobby would tell him about the conversation he'd just overheard. However, since that friendship had been put on hiatus, at the least, Bobby might as well find another confidant—even if he was Dean.

After relating what he'd heard, Dean pointed toward the main house. "Go get her."

"We're too different. Too driven."

"Doesn't being driven make you more the same?"

Dean was a lot smarter than he looked.

"I don't love her."

"You sure about that?"

"We've only known each other a few weeks. Less."

"You never even met Marlie, yet you were in love with her. But you can't be in love with a woman you shared a life-threatening adventure with? You've slept with Jane. You must feel something. You're not Evan."

They went silent, thinking about their littlest brother, who was the tallest of them all. Evan Luchetti had been the Luchetti family gigolo until he'd gone to Arkansas and discovered love in a haunted inn.

"Another one bites the dust," Dean murmured. "Only you and me left alone."

Alone.

Bobby didn't want to be. That was how the entire fiasco with Marlie had begun. He'd dreamed of something more. Could he have it with Jane? The idea wasn't as far-fetched as it should be.

Bear shot out of the cornfield. He skidded to a stop at the sight of the men on the porch. His head dipped to the ground and his shoulders hunched as his tail went between his legs.

Dean stood. "Not on your life, pal. Come here."

"What'd he do?"

"Nothing yet. He was on his way to the girlfriend's house."

"Mom said you had him fixed after the doodle incident."

"Yeah. But old dog, new tricks and all that. He still wanders. I keep him inside at night now. I don't want him to get shot for a coyote or hit by a truck."

Bear collapsed in a heap on the porch at Dean's feet, the picture of dejection, and silence settled over the land, as well as the porch.

This time was the best time on the farm. All the work was done, and there were hours before it would begin again. The moon shone on the cornfield, tingeing the floppy green leaves with silver. In the old days, farmers believed that the moon, not the sun, made things grow. On a night like this, with magic spilling from the sky, Bobby understood why.

"I've only met Marlie a few times," Dean murmured.

Bobby tensed, uncertain he wanted to hear this. Dean had met Marlie more than he had.

"But when Colin told me—"

Bobby glanced Dean's way, scowling, and Dean held up his hands in surrender. "Hey, don't beat the hell out of me, we're not twelve."

"*What* did he tell you?"

"About your argument." Dean shrugged. "I suddenly seem to be everyone's confidant. Probably because I'm the only one who stays put."

"What's your point?"

"She wasn't for you."

"Obviously."

"Listen for a minute, will you?" Dean took a deep breath. "Marlie's soft, sweet, easily freaked out. She's a preschool teacher from Minnesota."

"I know that, Dean."

"When Colin was kidnapped while he was searching for you, she nearly married another guy because— Well, she was pregnant, but that was beside the point."

Bobby clenched his hands. His idiot brother had gotten Marlie pregnant, then run off and tried to get himself killed in Pakistan. Even if Colin had been under the delusion Bobby needed rescuing, he still wanted to punch his brother in the face all over again.

"Marlie never would have survived your going back to Iraqistan."

"Afghanistan. Iraq. Gotta pick a country."

"*You* gotta see the truth. You would have had to choose between Marlie or the Special Forces. Were you prepared to do that?"

Bobby frowned. The army was his life. He hadn't planned on leaving.

"Aaron says everything happens for a reason. I always thought that was bull."

Bobby smiled. So had he.

"But the older I get the more sense it makes. Sometimes you don't see the why of it until later. Tim came here. He and I fit. We're good for each other. He needed me and I—"

Dean broke off, seeming to gather his thoughts.

"I needed someone," he finally admitted. "None of that would have happened if Aaron hadn't met a stripper fourteen years ago, screwed up his life, saved Nicole's, produced Rayne, who found Tim—"

"And everyone wound up here at the happy Luchetti insane asylum. Get to the point."

"I thought I had. Marlie wasn't for you, but Jane could be. She doesn't spook easily."

"I'll say."

"She's used to being on her own. She has an important job, which I doubt she wants to give up. You heard with your own ears she'd never ask you to give up yours. She's perfect, moron. So go get her before another one of your brothers beats you to it."

"There's only you left." Bobby narrowed his eyes. "Go near her and you'll wish you were never born."

"You won't be able to loosen my teeth as easily as Colin's," Dean said, but he was smiling.

Bobby couldn't help but smile back. Sometimes it was nice hanging out with a brother. Even if he was Dean.

Dean gave an exaggerated yawn, stretched and got to his feet. "Day begins early for me. You can take the couch."

He whistled for the dog, then strolled inside, waiting for Bear to get in, before letting the screen bang behind him.

"Couch, my ass," Bobby muttered.

He glanced toward the main house, where the

light shone in his and Colin's room like a beacon. Bear whimpered on the other side of the screen.

"Dean will have my head if I let you out."

Bear collapsed on the ground with a grumble and a sigh.

"I know. Sucks."

Bobby was still watching when the light in his room went out. Jane was lying in his old bed, hair spread across his pillow, long silky legs tangled in his sheets.

He glanced at Bear. Maybe wandering wasn't such a bad idea.

Bobby slipped off the porch and headed across the cornfield.

BOBBY'S MOTHER LOANED Jane a nightgown and some clothes for the next day. She even promised to buy Jane some new underwear and a bra in town. They were nearly the same size. Wasn't that just delightful?

She'd expected Bobby to say good-night. When he hadn't shown up by the time everyone was ready for bed, she went to bed, too.

Lying in the bottom bunk, with the window open and the sounds that darkness made drifting in, Jane fell asleep quickly and deeply. She'd always loved sleeping close to night.

She came awake, heart pounding, ears straining for the tiniest sound, and she wasn't sure why. The window was open, but she was on the second floor. Who was going to scale the side of a farmhouse?

"Bobby?" she whispered.

"How did you know?"

Since she hadn't really believed he was there, she gasped. He materialized from the corner of the room and sat on the bed.

"Your mother's going to kill us if she catches you in here."

"I know." He pulled off his shirt. The moon turned his skin silver, rippling over the dips and curves like a river over smooth stones. "Isn't it exciting?"

A nervous giggle escaped her lips. "You're crazy."

"About you."

Bobby leaned over and kissed her. Their kisses had been so few, she found herself mesmerized from the first taste.

When he lifted his head, she put her palm against his chest, holding him away. "What did you say?"

"I'm crazy about you, Jane. Can't you tell?"

"When you say crazy—"

"I mean, I don't want this to be a one-night stand."

Her fingers flexed, tracing his collarbone. "I think we passed one night about six or seven nights ago."

"You know what I mean." He laid his hand over hers. She felt his heart beating. His eyes picked up the glow from the moon and shone eerily pale in the night. "I want—"

Jane held her breath as he seemed to struggle with the words. She had no idea what he was going to say, but she wasn't going to interrupt him and make him forget to say it.

"You," he blurted out. "For more than a night, a weekend, a month. Can we see where this goes from here?"

A tiny shard of disappointment settled in Jane's chest. What had she expected? A declaration of everlasting love after only a couple of weeks?

Yes.

Bobby was waiting for her to say something. The idea of leaving here, leaving him, of never seeing Bobby Luchetti again was too depressing. Why *couldn't* they see where this went? Maybe it would go exactly where she wanted it to.

Where's that? her conscience asked in Raeanne's voice. *To a baby for you and a shallow grave in another country for him?*

Jane winced.

"Bad idea," Bobby murmured, and inched away. "No."

She pulled him back, and kept pulling until his entire body rested on top of hers. He nuzzled her ear, nibbled her earlobe, and she tried to concentrate on the subject. He was making it awfully difficult.

Bobby hadn't declared love. He hadn't proposed marriage. He wanted to continue their affair. And wasn't that exactly what she'd always said she wanted from a man?

A physical relationship. No strings. A little sperm and voilà. Baby Harker.

No wonder her mother thought she was cold.

As Bobby's kisses became more demanding and his body became as hard as the questions, Jane had to wonder if perhaps marriage wasn't such a bad idea—if she married Bobby.

He'd lived in a household where his parents had

enjoyed an equal and loving relationship. Bobby would want to continue his job, so he'd be supportive of Jane continuing hers. They could have a perfect life. If he loved her.

And when had she decided she needed love? Maybe she just needed it from him.

"Jane?"

"Mmm?" She kissed his jaw.

"You never answered me."

"What was the question?" she stalled.

"I don't want this to end when you go back to Mexico, or wherever it is you're going."

"Mexico," she said.

"We could meet somewhere, or I could take leaves and come to you."

"You'd travel halfway across the world for great sex?"

"No." He brushed her hair out of her face. "For you."

Her eyes burned. "That's probably the nicest thing anyone's ever said to me."

"Then I'll have to be nicer." He kissed her. "Is that a yes?"

Jane stared into Bobby's eyes and knew the truth. She couldn't give him up. Not now. Not ever.

She loved him, and sooner or later he would love her. They'd work everything out. Together.

"That's a yes," she answered, and then there was no more talking for the rest of the night.

CHAPTER SIXTEEN

THE SUN SPILLED THROUGH the window and across Bobby's face. Someone's legs were all tangled with his. Hair was stuck to his lip. He spit it out and remembered.

Jane.

Smiling without even opening his eyes, he tugged her naked body closer and snuggled.

"You forgot Marlie pretty damn quick, bro."

Bobby's eyes shot open. Colin leaned over the bed, staring at him in disgust.

Jane gasped and tore the covers away, leaving Bobby buck naked to face his brother, which might have been a little bit easier without his morning hardon.

He glanced at Colin's face.

Then again, maybe not. Bobby grabbed a pillow and laid it in his lap as he sat up. Jane put her head under the covers and moaned.

"What the hell are you doing here?" Bobby demanded.

"In Illinois or in this room?"

"Both."

"Same reason. I want to talk to you."

"I don't want to talk to you."

"You have to. Mom said."

Bobby snorted. "How did you know where I was?"

"Dean called. Told me if I wanted to make nicey-nice I should get home before you disappeared again. He didn't mention..." Colin nodded in the direction of Jane's rump.

Dean, the traitor. Bobby was going to kick his ass just on principle. Whoever taught him to be a confidant?

"Jane," Bobby murmured.

"Go away!" she whispered furiously.

"Me? Or him?"

"Both of you. This is mortifying!"

"Why?"

"How did he know you were here? You're supposed to be at Dean's."

Bobby glanced at Colin, who shrugged. "Mom."
Jane moaned again.

"The woman knows everything," Colin muttered.

"Maybe you should take a shower." Bobby patted Jane's back. He didn't want her to witness what he and Colin were about to say.

"I'll just stay under here until I die, thanks."

Bobby laughed and rubbed her shoulders. "Come on, Doctor, everything'll look better once you're wearing clothes."

She gave a labored sigh and poked her head out. Bobby smiled and kissed her nose. He was pleased to see her smile back, until her gaze shifted to his brother. Then uncertainty filtered over her face.

He hated that expression. Jane was the most certain person he knew.

"Jane, that's Colin. Ignore him. Sometimes it works."

"Not this time." Colin nodded politely at Jane. "Nice to meet you."

"Likewise."

Jane got to her feet, wrapping the bedspread around her, before she snatched her clothes from the floor. Then she hurried out the door, nearly tripping over the tail end. Bobby wanted to go after her so badly he took a step in that direction.

Colin moved in front of him. "We're going to settle this once and for all."

"There's nothing to settle."

"You come to our house, upset Marlie, tell me I stole your girl and disappear. Then you turn up with another woman and think everything's hunky-dory? I thought you were desperately in love with my wife."

Bobby had thought he was, too.

"This woman—" Colin began.

"Jane."

"What are you playing at? Evan's married so you have to be the new gigolo? Forget Marlie in the arms of anyone you can find? And what's with bringing her home, screwing her under your parents' roof?"

Bobby's fingers curled into fists. No one talked about Jane that way—not even his brother.

"It isn't like that."

"What's it like, then? You love Marlie. Your life is over because you can't have her. The next thing I know you're here with a stranger."

"She's not a stranger."

"Not anymore." Colin glanced pointedly at the bed. "Obviously."

"You have no idea what you're talking about, so *stop* talking before I knock out a few more of your teeth."

"That's your answer for everything, isn't it?"

"It's worked pretty well so far."

"Fine." Colin pointed to his chin. "Hit me again if it'll make you feel better. I just want my brother back."

"You can't always get what you want."

"Now you sound like Mom." Colin took a deep breath. "I didn't know you loved Marlie. Hell, she didn't even know it. We didn't mean—"

"I know."

"Thinking of her was what kept me sane when I was in that cell. Being with her now is the only way I can stop remembering what it was like."

"You shouldn't have come searching for me."

"But I did."

They went silent, thinking of what might have happened in Pakistan, then remembering what had.

"How could you love her?" Colin asked. "You never even met her."

Bobby didn't want to explain his life. How lonely it could get sometimes. How desperate he was to have someone waiting for him somewhere.

How pathetic was that? It wasn't as if he didn't love his job, didn't believe in what he was doing. He didn't want to leave the Special Forces, he only wanted to have a life outside of it. So he'd latched onto the first woman he thought he could make a future with and convinced himself he was in love with her.

He hadn't been. Bobby could see that now. Because he was in love with Jane.

"Hold on." He headed for the hall, no longer caring he was naked, only caring that he found her.

However, Colin wasn't going to surrender easily. He put a hand on Bobby's chest and shoved. Bobby grabbed his wrist and twisted.

Colin's breath hissed in sharply. "I hate it when you do that."

"Then get out of my way. I need to talk to Jane."

"Now?"

"I love her."

"Sheesh. Make up your mind."

"I have."

Everything was completely clear. He wanted Jane for more than a day, a week, a month. He wanted her forever. Why hadn't he told her so last night?

Since he'd found Jane in the jungle, he hadn't felt lonely, he'd felt…complete. She was the other half he'd been searching for when he hadn't even known he was searching.

Bobby walked down the hall, Colin on his heels. Something was bothering him, and he couldn't figure out what until he neared the bathroom and didn't hear the shower running. The door was open; Jane wasn't inside.

"Jane!" he bellowed, and ran for the stairs.

Colin snagged one arm, and Bobby swung at him with the other. Colin ducked. He always had been quick. "You might want to try pants first."

Bobby glanced down. "Good idea."

Ninety seconds later he burst into the kitchen. His mother was there. So were Dean, Tim, his dad.

But not Jane.

"Did you two get everything worked out?" Eleanor glanced over her shoulder as she stirred scrambled eggs.

"Where's Jane?"

His mother frowned. "She isn't with you?"

Bobby's gaze went to the window. Their car was gone.

"She heard us," Bobby muttered.

Colin cast him a quick glance. "She didn't know about Marlie?"

"Hell, no. You think I'm an idiot?"

Something smacked him in the forehead out of nowhere. Scrambled eggs sprayed all over his chest. Tim giggled.

"Gramma hit him with the spatula. Big trouble."

Bobby turned to his mother, who held her cooking utensil as if she'd use it on him again.

"You *are* an idiot. That girl is the best thing that ever happened to you. Find her, beg her to love you, then marry her. Preferably today."

"Yes, ma'am."

His mother blinked, then stared at her spatula. "Wow, this thing really works."

Bobby headed out the front door, Colin right behind him.

"Where do you think you're going?"

"With you."

"I don't know where I'm going."

Bobby stared up the lane, hoping against hope he'd see a trail of dust from Jane's car that would give him a hint, but there was nothing.

"Where would she go?"

"Mexico."

"You think you can catch her before she gets there?"

Canine grumbling erupted an instant before Lucky pressed against Bobby's leg. The panic that had been making it hard for him to breathe eased as he went down on one knee and accepted some Lucky love.

"*What* is that?" Colin demanded.

"Jane's dog."

"I wouldn't sound so happy about it if I were you."

"She's coming back. She'd never leave Lucky."

"You sure?"

"I'm sure," Bobby said, and sat on the porch to wait.

I THOUGHT YOU WERE desperately in love with my wife.

Jane kept hearing Colin's words even as she heard Bobby's silence, which spoke even louder.

No wonder he hadn't declared his everlasting love. He'd already given it to someone else. That's what she got for dreaming of forever.

Jane drove over unfamiliar gravel roads far too fast. She wasn't exactly sure where she was going, except away from him.

Eventually she'd be forced to return to the farm. She'd left Lucky behind. The dog hadn't been anywhere easy to find without shouting, and Jane hadn't wanted to alert every Luchetti in the vicinity to her plans.

At the next farm over, she slowed. The sign on the mailbox read Riley. Jane swung into the drive. Bobby's sister *had* begged her to visit.

Expecting another assault of Dalmatians, if not doodles, Jane was surprised when she was able to climb out of the car unmolested. That didn't last long.

A black sheep with a cat riding shotgun trotted around the side of the house.

"Baaaaa."

"Likewise, I'm sure." Jane started for the front door.

The sheep put her head down as if she planned to charge.

"Hey!" Jane shouted. "I come in peace."

The front door opened and Kim appeared, Zsa-Zsa hanging on to her leg.

"No, Ba!" Zsa-Zsa said sternly. "No."

"Sorry." Kim let the screen door bang shut. "Ba doesn't like strangers."

Jane could have figured that out from the cranky expression on the ewe's face, if not her continued precharging position.

"Shoo, Ba. Shoo," Kim said.

The sheep snorted in disgust and trotted around the side of the house, cat still clinging to her back like a jockey.

"You named your sheep Ba?" Jane asked.

That seemed a little unimaginative for a woman like Kim—even if she was an almost-lawyer.

"Not me. Brian."

"The cat isn't Meow, is it?"

"No, it's—"

"Precious!" Zsa-Zsa shouted, and took off after the animals.

Jane lifted a brow.

"I was out of my mind at the time," Kim muttered. "Come on in."

Jane hesitated, but where was she going to go? The Luchetti farm? Right now, she just couldn't.

"Coffee?" Kim asked.

"Thanks."

The kitchen was trashed. Cereal lay all over the table and across the floor. Law books and loose paper covered the countertop.

"Sorry. I'm afraid you've arrived on the maid's year off."

Jane smiled. "You should see my place."

"Where's that?"

"Hut in the jungle. Real mess."

Kim laughed and poured Jane some coffee.

"What brings you to my lovely home so bright and early this morning?"

Jane stared at her feet and fought the urge to cry. Crying was so unlike her…it made Jane want to cry.

"Sit." Kim set the coffee on the table, then cleared a space in front of two chairs. "What did my idiot brother do?"

Jane snuffled and took the seat next to Kim. "Which one?"

"I assume Bobby, but you're right. Could be any of them. Spill it."

"He doesn't love me. He loves her."

Jane glanced at Kim in time to catch the truth flitting across her face.

"You knew. All of you did." Jane fought the mortification. "From the moment I showed up, everyone but me understood he couldn't love me. He was only using me." Jane stood. "I have to go."

"No." Kim put a hand on Jane's. "Let's talk."

"Why? Will he suddenly fall out of love with his brother's wife and make a life with me?"

Kim sighed and tugged on her arm. Though Jane outweighed her by a good seventy pounds, she gave in and sat.

"How did you find out?" Kim asked.

"Colin came by."

Jane decided to leave out the part where Colin had caught them in bed.

"Oh-oh," Kim muttered.

"What?"

Kim hesitated an instant, then shrugged. "The last time those two were together, Bobby loosened a few of Colin's teeth."

"Over Marlie?"

"Yeah."

Jane sighed. "I suppose she's beautiful. Small like you. Thin. Blond."

"You got blond. But Marlie's...well, Marlie. She's soft, sweet. She likes to have babies, take care of people, stay home and make cookies."

Jane frowned. Marlie didn't sound like Bobby's type at all.

"It's a long story," Kim said.

"So tell it fast."

Kim considered Jane for a few seconds, and then she began to speak. When she finished, they were silent. Zsa-Zsa's laughter rang from the backyard. Every once in a while Ba would *ba*. In the distance a tractor hummed, revealing Brian Riley was hard at work somewhere else.

"You aren't going to give up on him, are you?" Kim asked.

"Yes," Jane said. "I think I am."

In Mexico, she'd believed her life was perfect. She didn't need a man, she only wanted for a child. Then Bobby had snuck in and shown her what she'd been lacking.

She'd miss him forever, but she wasn't going to waste time or energy waiting for a love that would never come. There were people in the world who needed her.

"It's been great meeting you. We should keep in touch."

Jane headed for the door and Kim scrambled after her. "But—"

"No buts. Bobby never promised love. He couldn't. But I'm not begging for it, either."

She'd wished for her father's love, begged for her mother's, and it hadn't done her any good at all.

"Where are you going?" Kim asked.

"I'm getting my dog, and then I'm going home."

As they reached the front of the house, Ba bleated loudly, and then she wouldn't stop.

"Someone's here," Kim murmured. "Someone Ba doesn't like."

"Does she like anyone?"

"Not really."

Kim glanced out the window next to the door. "I don't know him."

Absently, Jane glanced outside, too. A trickle of unease filtered down her spine. "I do."

Something wasn't right here, and if Jane had learned one thing in the past few weeks, it was that it was better to err on the side of caution.

Kim reached for the door and Jane stopped her. "Go out the back. Grab Zsa-Zsa. Get Brian and go to your parents. Do not let Brian come here. You understand? Get Bobby."

"But—"

The doorbell rang.

"We don't have time to argue," Jane whispered.

Kim stared into Jane's eyes, and then she ran.

Jane waited as long as she could before opening the door.

JANE DIDN'T COME BACK, and Bobby had been so sure that she would. Where had she gone?

His family finished breakfast. Dean went to work and took Colin, which would be amusing if Bobby felt like laughing. Colin had arrived wearing gray silk slacks, a crisp white shirt and shiny black shoes, which weren't going to be shiny for very long.

John went to town and took Tim. Bobby's mother kept going to the door and muttering "Moron" before returning to the kitchen.

"You're not helping!" he shouted when she did it for the tenth time.

Lucky and Bull trotted up, took one look at him and collapsed at his feet. Bobby stared at the two of them for a long minute. Lucky lay with her neck over Bull's. They were awfully cuddly.

"Did you get Bull fixed along with Bear?" he called.

His mother appeared on the other side of the screen. "No. Remember, Bull's a little backward. When we tried to breed him that one time, he didn't get it."

"Seems like he's getting it now."

Eleanor followed Bobby's gaze.

"Hell," she said, and stomped into the kitchen.

"Where would she go?" Bobby asked the dogs.

They merely sighed, cuddled closer and remained silent.

His mother came back. "She's at Kim's."

Bobby jumped to his feet. "Kim called?"

"No. I just know these things."

She turned away, and he was left wondering if she'd been serious or not. He was never really sure.

Bobby snapped his fingers and the dogs lifted their heads. "Car ride."

Bull ran toward the pickup trucks. Lucky followed. Bobby decided to borrow Colin's. His brother had conveniently left the keys in the ignition. Colin was going to have a fit when he saw all the dog hair, which made taking it worthwhile.

Bobby headed up the lane, then down the road. Both dogs hung their heads out of the window and drooled down the side of the sparkling black pickup. Colin would have a stroke.

Bobby discovered he was grinning. Everything was going to work out fine.

He'd find Jane, declare his love, then they'd pack up their stuff, including Lucky, elope and…

He wasn't quite sure. He'd cross that bridge once he convinced Jane she couldn't live without him.

Bobby turned into the driveway next to the sign that read Riley. Jane's car was there. So were Brian's, Kim's and another he didn't recognize.

He wasn't wild about declaring his love in front of a stranger, but whatever it took.

Bobby climbed out and released the dogs. They ran off immediately—probably to make doggy love behind the barn. He didn't relish informing Jane that they were probably going to be grandparents. He wondered what flavor of dogs Lucky and Bull were going to make. Doodles were cute but—

He thought of Lucky and shuddered.

Expecting Kim to come out of the house, he frowned when everything remained quiet. Too quiet, in fact. Where was Ba? The watch sheep was more vigilant than any dog. He hoped she hadn't died during the years he'd been away. Ba might be cranky, but he liked her.

The place was far too silent for the amount of cars in the yard. Bobby climbed the porch and knocked. He didn't hear a sound, so he tried the knob, which turned easily in his hand.

Calling Jane's name, Bobby stepped inside.

CHAPTER SEVENTEEN

JANE DECIDED GREG WYLIE was a can short of a six-pack even before he tied her to a pole in the hay mow and began to tell her all of his crimes.

As soon as she'd opened the door, he'd walked right in and grabbed her, not even bothering to pretend he was there on an errand from her mother.

"Where's the rest of them?" he demanded.

"Gone."

He shook Jane so hard she felt as if her neck would snap.

Here we go again, she thought. *And my black eyes just went away.*

"You think I'm an idiot? There are too many cars here for you to be alone."

"They're working in the far field. Won't be back until lunch."

He stared into her eyes. Gone was the suave politician. He'd kill her and he wouldn't even care. But why?

Greg dragged Jane through the entire house, making sure no one was there, then he dragged her to the barn.

Using some twine from a bale of hay, he tied her to one of the support poles.

"I thought I was going to have to shoot that sheep," he muttered. "Thing went nuts, then it just took off."

Jane hoped Ba had followed Kim to the Luchettis'. That would be one less thing to worry about.

"What's going on?" Jane asked.

"We're waiting for a phone call. If Mommy follows instructions, you live. If not—" He shrugged and pulled a gun from his suit coat.

So Raeanne *was* being blackmailed. Trust her mother to lie.

"How did you find me?" she asked.

"The senator wants me to marry you." His lip curled at the very idea. "She wheedled Luchetti's home address out of someone—I'm not sure how—then all I had to do was ask."

Nice one, Mom.

Greg shook his head. "As if I'd marry a woman who outweighed me, even if her mother is a senator."

Jane would have flipped him off if her hands weren't tied.

"How did you find me *here?*" she asked.

"Followed you from the other farm. It wasn't hard."

Nice one, me.

"What is my mother supposed to do for you?"

"Vote in favor of relaxing the immigration laws."

"Okay." Jane searched her memory banks for a

reason this would matter to Greg. She came up blank. "I don't get it."

"From what I hear, you've been getting it quite a lot. And from a common soldier." He shook his head. "How low can you go?"

"Lower, I suppose, but only if I sleep with you."

He snorted. "As if that'll happen."

"Got that right."

Greg's lips tightened. He pulled out his cell phone and checked the display, before returning it to his coat and aiming his gun at her chest. "You know, I'm almost hoping she votes against it."

"What did I ever do to you?" Jane asked.

"You embarrassed me in front of the entire town. Washington may be large, but in political circles, it's really quite small. Everyone knew you were supposed to marry me. Then you turn up sleeping with the bodyguard, frenching him right on the dance floor in front of three-quarters of Congress. It was mortifying."

"But you don't *want* to marry me."

Greg sniffed. "That's beside the point."

Jane decided he was *several* cans short of that six-pack.

"I still don't understand why you care about an immigration bill."

"The more wetbacks allowed in, the more drugs that can be smuggled in with them."

"You're a drug dealer?" Jane blurted out.

She hadn't seen that coming. Where was Lucky when she needed her?

"What did you think I was?"

"An aide to the senator from Rhode Island."

"Which doesn't pay very well. Drugs are where the money is."

"Does my mother know any of this?"

"She's too preoccupied with her career, and she trusts me. She'd never consider that her right-hand man is the one screwing with her life."

"My mother thought I was going to be kidnapped."

"You were. But then she just had to have Delray send someone after you. Pissed me off. So I told them to kill you instead."

Well, that explained a little. Greg was the rich American who had paid to have her eliminated. Still—

"If Enrique or Escobar had killed me, you wouldn't have had any leverage with my mother."

"Of course we would. She'd have been scared shitless thinking we'd come for her next."

He had a point.

"Someone's going to figure this out eventually."

"By then I'll be lounging on a beach in a country without extradition laws. Politics is almost as big of a pain as your mother."

Jane suddenly understood, even if Greg didn't yet, that he planned to kill her, anyway, regardless of whether Raeanne did the right—or was it the wrong?—thing or not. He was being far too forthcoming with the info. Jane had to keep him talking, and she had to think.

"You've known what she was doing every step of the way?" Jane asked.

"Of course. I'm her only friend. She tells me everything."

"Escobar kept asking about Bobby as if he didn't know who he was or why he was there."

"Your mother didn't tell me right away that she'd sent in the troops—or is that troop? I only had time to get in touch with Enrique. When word got out that a soldier was snooping around, Escobar Senior, being the paranoid SOB that he is, got it in his head that the captain was there to kill him."

Greg pulled his phone out of his pocket and glanced at the display again. He really couldn't wait to kill her.

"And then?" Jane prompted.

"Then he got all spooked and ordered his son—who was basically an idiot—to find out what was going on. Once I heard Luchetti was bringing you back to the States, I called off the hit. Figured I could take care of you here all by myself."

"*You* shot at me?"

The dreamy expression fled as extreme annoyance took its place. "Weren't you listening when we danced? I earned a gold medal in the biathlon."

She hadn't been listening, and she really wasn't sure what a biathlon was, which must have shown on her face since Greg made a disgusted sound and snapped, "Skiing and sharpshooting?"

"Ah, well that explains it, then. Although you missed."

His hand tightened on the gun. "I won't miss at this range."

"Lucky wouldn't miss at this range," she muttered.

"Your mother made everything so easy. Insisting you go to that ball so she could shove it in her blackmailer's face that you were alive and no one could hurt you."

Her mother's arrogance had forever been a problem.

"But since I planned the thing, I had clearance. I brought my rifle inside in pieces. Then reassembled it after the final security check and hid it in the balcony."

Greg started and his hand went to his pocket. He removed the cell phone, which must have been set to vibrate instead of ring. A glance at the display, and he allowed a thin smile to escape before he answered the call.

Whoever was on the other end spoke. Greg listened, turned off the phone, dropped the instrument back into his pocket and contemplated Jane. "Your mother doesn't love you very much, does she?"

Jane had always suspected her mother loved her country, or at least the power she got from serving it, more, but she'd never really been sure.

Greg pointed the gun at Jane's head.

Until now.

The sound of a car crackling over gravel outside the barn split the silence and Greg cursed, then pocketed the weapon.

Jane opened her mouth to shout, but snapped it shut again when she considered the car might not be the cavalry, aka Bobby, but some poor sap who'd come to visit the Rileys. She couldn't put anyone in danger.

Greg yanked a handkerchief from his pocket and gagged Jane. She only hoped he was the kind of man who carried a handkerchief for show and not for snot.

"Stay there," he said, then snickered at his wit, before slipping out of the barn.

The instant he was gone, Jane began to pick at the fraying twine around her wrists. Greg was almost as bad at tying knots as he was at being Prince Charming.

BOBBY HAD JUST STEPPED out of the house and onto the porch when a creak from the barn made him turn.

A tall, thin, familiar blond man in a suit and wire-rimmed glasses crossed the yard. "Hello, Luchetti."

"Wylie," Bobby said. "What are you doing here?"

"I brought Jane's things. You know how women are."

He did, and Jane wasn't like any of them.

"And how did you know where Jane was?"

"You know the senator—"

"Not really."

"Well, she's very persuasive. She exerted all the pressure she had to get the colonel to tell her where her child was. The man didn't stand a chance once she set her mind to it."

Bobby frowned. That wasn't like the colonel.

"Long way to travel to bring things that could have been shipped."

"Her mother wanted me to see with my own trusty eyes how her daughter was. The senator's like that."

Bobby could well imagine. He only hoped this guy wasn't as stupid as he looked and hadn't led the bad guys right to their doorstep. So far, so good. But as soon as Bobby found Jane, they were out of here. He wasn't taking any chances.

"Funny thing," Wylie continued. "I was headed for your farm and I saw Jane turn in the driveway. Of course, there aren't exactly a bevy of people on these roads."

What was a bevy?

"Where is she?" Bobby asked.

"Something about heavy machinery in the back field."

He pointed to the north and Bobby followed his finger. Brian's tractor sat idle on the other side of the corn.

The two men stared at each other. There was something off about Wylie, but then there always had been. Maybe Bobby was just irritated with the man because Wylie had the mistaken impression he had a shot in hell with Jane.

Kim's phone started to ring inside the house, breaking the silent spell.

"I guess I'll head to the back field," Bobby said. "I suspect you'd like to get on the road."

"I would. Nice seeing you again."

Bobby grunted in lieu of a lie and started toward the tractor. He'd only taken one step when Lucky's drug-dealer snarl split the warm sunny peace of the morning.

Everything became very clear—even before Wylie pulled a gun from his pocket and aimed it at Lucky.

Undaunted, she continued to snarl. Bull, usually the king of the wusseys, charged out of nowhere and joined her. Confusion flickered over Wylie's face. Which dog should he shoot first?

"I wouldn't," Bobby said, and the gun was aimed in his direction.

Bobby had a gun, too. Unfortunately, he wasn't going to be able to retrieve it from the glove compartment anytime soon. He hadn't thought he'd need it on his sister's farm, but he should have known better. Then again, he wasn't going to need a gun to kick this guy's ass.

"Where is she?" Bobby demanded for the second time.

"I'll take you to her. You want to die together, fine by me."

Wylie jerked his head toward the barn and Lucky lunged at him. The gun swung in her direction and Bobby shouted, "No!"

He started to run across the ground that separated them, but contrary to his own high opinion of himself, Bobby wasn't faster than a speeding bullet.

However, Jane was. Like an avenging angel, she

flew out of the barn. Instead of a lightning bolt, she held a two-by-four. Before Wylie could do anything but smirk, she beaned him over the head. He went down and he didn't get up.

"Shoot my dog?" she sneered. "I don't think so."

Lucky stopped growling and belly-crawled to Jane. Bobby was so damn glad to see her, he almost did the same thing.

Bull leaped with excitement. Jane snapped, "Sit!" and when he did, she burst into tears.

"Hey!" Alarmed, Bobby ran to her. "Did he hurt you?"

His gaze searched her face—not a mark. His hands moved over her head—not a bump. He'd have to get her naked and check for bruises.

She shoved him in the chest, and he stumbled back, nearly falling on top of Wylie.

"I'm fine," she said. "If being fine involves discovering my mother sold me down the river to keep her job."

"What?"

"Never mind," she said. "Suffice it to say no one loves me. Big shock."

"I love you."

She gave him a withering glare, hefted the two-by-four and said, "Do not make me use this on you, soldier boy."

Then she whistled to the dogs and headed for the car. Bobby would have followed her, except Wylie began to stir. While he tied the man with the twine that had trailed out of the barn on Jane's shoe, she started the engine and drove away.

"That went well," he commented to a semiconscious Wylie.

JANE HAD NEVER BEEN SO furious or so sad. The conflicting emotions had her stomach roiling and her tear ducts working overtime. She didn't even slow down as a pickup truck full of Luchettis armed with rifles and farm implements whooshed past. Kim and the children had apparently remained at the other farm.

The police sped by as she turned into the Luchettis'. They ignored her, intent on reaching the action at the next farm. Too bad for them it was already over. Just like her and Bobby.

Jane's breath hitched, and Lucky licked her from chin to cheek.

"Thanks, girl. I'll be okay."

And she would be. As soon as she got back to Mexico and forgot him.

"Like that'll happen."

Nevertheless, she was going. Bobby didn't love her, and she wasn't going to believe that he did just because he said so in the heat of the moment.

Jane parked in front of the house. Bear and the doodles welcomed her, along with Ba and Precious, but the rest of the place was deserted. Confused, she went inside and found a note from Kim.

We cut across the cornfield.

Trust Kim not to sit home and wait for news.

"I need to make some time."

Jane wanted out of here before any of the Luchettis tried to make her stay. Now that no one wanted to kill her, as far as she knew, she could head back to the jungle and disappear.

CHAPTER EIGHTEEN

"SHE'S A DOGNAPPER," Dean said. "There's no other word for it."

They'd returned to the farm to discover not only Jane gone, but Lucky and Bull, as well.

"Bull loves Lucky and Lucky loves Bull," Tim announced. "They're gonna have mutations."

"Probably," John muttered. Colin just shook his head.

"Mutt plus Dalmatian makes a mutation." Tim's too-long hair slid over one eye. "Right?"

Dean clapped a hand on his son's shoulder. "Right."

The police had carted off Wylie, who had begun to blabber information in an attempt to offset kidnapping and murder charges. Bobby didn't think he could talk long enough or loud enough to get out of either one.

Who'd have thought a weasel like Wylie would be operating one of the largest drug rings on the East Coast? Senator Harker was going to have to do some fancy dancing if she didn't want that dirt to rub off on her.

"I can't understand," Eleanor said for perhaps the fourth time, "how a mother could choose…well, anything over the safety of her child."

"That's because you're a great mother," Kim said. "Some aren't."

She gathered a sleeping Zsa-Zsa closer and kissed her sweaty brow, then reached up to grasp Brian's hand. Their fingers laced in a pattern that fit together like a jigsaw puzzle. Bobby wanted what they had so badly he ached with it.

"Gotta go," he said.

"What?" Eleanor asked. "Where?"

"She said she was going home," Kim offered.

"Which means Mexico."

"Maybe you should call Jane's mother first," his own mother suggested.

"Why?" There was no way Jane considered anywhere near her mother a place to call home. "So I can yell at her?"

Which wasn't a half-bad idea. Bobby headed for the phone in the living room—he didn't feel like having this conversation in front of his entire family.

"All hell's breaking loose here," the senator snapped. "What happened?"

"It appears you sold your only child's life for a good voting record."

"I should have been able to vote my conscience and save my child. I hired you to protect Jane."

"Jane saved herself. She didn't need any help from me."

"She's always been very good at that."

"Unfortunately, she thinks you chose politics over her."

A fluid stream of curses erupted. The senator really needed to improve her vocabulary.

"Next time you choose an aide, make sure he isn't a drug dealer," Bobby suggested.

"He didn't actually do the deals. He managed things."

"Oh, well that's different, then," Bobby said.

"There's a lot worse going on in Washington than drug dealing."

"Is that the line you plan to use on CNN?"

Raeanne sighed. "I screwed up."

"Yep."

"Do you know where my daughter is?"

"No idea."

Which wasn't technically a lie. Mexico was a very big place.

"Can't you find her? I'll pay you—"

"I'll find Jane for me, not for you."

Instead of colorful language, silence came over the line, then, "She won't marry you."

"Excuse me?"

"My daughter has made it very clear she wants a child and not a husband. Ask anyone who knows her."

"I don't understand."

"She loves children, but she doesn't trust men. I blame her father."

No kidding. As if the senator would ever see that

her own behavior had made Jane as suspicious of love and commitment as any betrayal by a father she could barely remember. But he had a feeling telling Raeanne that would be like banging his head against cement.

Been there, done that, with a little help from his brothers; he didn't want to do it again.

"Don't be surprised if she's pregnant when you find her."

"She's on the pill."

"Except for when you were on the run through the jungle and left them behind. She had me refill her prescription when she got to D.C."

Now Bobby was the one who cursed.

"I didn't understand why she was so interested in you. Then it hit me."

"Why don't you hit me with it?"

"You're big and strong, nice-looking, and from what I've been able to gather, pretty damn smart for a farm boy. Excellent gene pool. With the added plus that you're out of the country most of the time, and there's a very good chance that one day you won't return."

Bobby frowned. He couldn't see Jane being so cold-blooded. Although she *had* lied to him about the birth control.

If she loved him, would she have taken off without a goodbye? He wasn't sure.

Bobby hung up on the senator, then wandered back into the kitchen with everyone else.

"What did she say?" Kim asked.

He told them.

"Bullshit," Kim said.

"Bull*shit!*" Zsa-Zsa shouted, suddenly wide awake.

"Great," Brian murmured, and took the little girl outside.

"You believe her?" Kim asked.

"Doesn't matter."

"Because?"

He met his sister's eyes. "I love her, anyway."

Kim grinned. "I knew she was the one the minute I saw her."

"Could have informed me."

"That would only have made you mad. You thought you were in love with Marlie."

"Who?"

Colin stepped forward. "You want me to take you to the airport?"

"Yeah."

"We okay?"

"Were we not okay?"

Colin tested his teeth. "You punched me in the mouth just for fun?"

"I always do."

BOBBY HAD A HELLUVA time finding her.

He called the Doctors of Mercy, but, according to them, Jane was on a leave of absence. No matter what he said, they wouldn't give him any more information than that. So he made use of his training and started the hunt.

Jane hadn't taken public transportation. Bobby figured she must have conned someone with a private plane into flying her back to Mexico.

Lucky for him, he discovered Escobar had met his demise in the form of a coup by one of his minions. Bobby was able to return to Mexico without worrying the man was still after him.

He returned to the village where he'd found Jane, but she was gone. No one knew where. Or at least they said they didn't. He didn't have enough Spanish in his repertoire to threaten them adequately, even if he'd had the heart for it.

Every time he was ready to give up, he remembered her face, her laughter, her strength. Bobby believed Jane loved him, and he wasn't going to let that disappear into the jungle forever—especially if she was carrying their child.

Of course she'd never *said* she loved him, but if she didn't, then why was she so mad? Or at least that's what Kim told him every time he called her in despair.

"Nothing worth having is easy," she said, and Bobby knew she was right.

The colonel contacted him regularly, trying to get Bobby to save the world again. But without Jane to come home to, the world could rot. He needed her.

Eventually word trickled through the jungle of a very ugly, hugely pregnant one-eyed dog and her spotted cohort. Bobby followed the trail to another village and another hut.

He arrived in the dead of night. The place was silent, still. Which hut was hers?

He crept into town, determined to search every dwelling until he found her, but he didn't have to. A familiar grumbling sounded an instant before something furry erupted from the shadows.

Lucky pressed against his leg. Bull leaped in three-foot-high leaps.

"At least someone loves me," Bobby whispered, and gave them both a pat.

Lucky was no longer bone thin or mangy. Her coat glowed with health, and her belly swayed nearly to the ground.

"You look like you're about to pop," he said.

She tossed her head, then waddled over and collapsed in front of the third hut on his left. Bull joined her, curling around Lucky's back and tucking his snout beneath her ear. They both ignored Bobby as he stepped inside the hut.

His gaze went to the bed. The lump beneath the blanket was suspiciously round and his heart lurched. Was Jane as pregnant as Lucky?

Bobby hurried across the dirt floor and flipped back the cover to reveal—

Pillows.

"How did you find me?"

Her voice came out of the night. Bobby turned and caught the glitter of her eyes from a corner of the room. At least this time she didn't have a knife— or at least he hoped she didn't.

"Finding is what I do."

"Since when?"

"Since you left."

She moved forward, into the moonlight that shone through the hole in the hut that served as a window. He couldn't help it, his gaze went to her stomach, and his breath rushed out in a relieved sigh.

She wasn't pregnant—at least not yet. Not that he didn't want her to be someday. But their child should be created purposefully, not by accident. Although, according to her mother, it wouldn't have been an accident.

She noticed his glance and his reaction. "You spoke to Raeanne, obviously."

"Of course. She was worried."

"I knew my big mouth would come back to haunt me. You can rest easy, Luchetti. There won't be any little Luchettis running around the jungle."

Did he detect sadness in her voice? Maybe she loved him, after all.

"Your mother was just trying to make me quit searching for you, but she doesn't know me very well."

"She was telling the truth."

"She said you wanted a baby without the husband."

"I did. I mean, I *do*."

"You lied to me?"

"Yes. No. Hell."

He stifled a smile as she repeated the words he always used when confused. "Which is it?"

"I was on the pill—until you dragged me into the jungle and I left them behind."

"But—"

"But I got some new ones, toot sweet, and you're safe, Bobby. You don't have to worry about me. So go back to saving the world. I don't need you."

He winced. She didn't need him, but he definitely needed her.

"You should have told me," he said.

"Why, when there was a very slim chance I'd wind up pregnant?"

"A slim chance is usually all it takes."

"Not this time."

"I hurt you," he said. "I didn't meant to."

"I know."

Silence descended. They stared at each other. He wasn't sure what to say, how to begin.

"What do you want?" she whispered.

"You."

"You had me, Bobby. Several times. Go back to the woman you love."

"I did."

She flinched, and he realized she thought he'd gone to Marlie.

"You're here," he blurted. "I mean she's you. Damn. I'm no good at this."

"At what?"

"I love you."

She shook her head. "You're off the hook, Luchetti. No baby. From what I hear, my mother's so busy trying to save her own neck, she isn't going to have time to screw up your life just for kicks. And if the colonel is giving you trouble, send him to me. I'll make sure everything's okay."

"The only way everything's going to be okay is if you marry me."

"I heard you and Colin. You love his wife."

"I did. Or I thought I did. Until I met you."

"Spare me. I don't need a man who can't make up his mind. I've had one of those. His name was Dad."

"I didn't even know Marlie," he said. "I wanted someone. Needed something."

"You were lonely. Probably horny. So was I. But you don't love me."

"Quit telling me what I feel."

Desperate, furious, a little bit scared—what would he do if she never believed him?—Bobby yanked Jane into his arms and kissed her.

At first she stood stiff and unresponsive. Her lips were warm, yet she tasted so cold. Her eyes wide open, she was creeping him out. She pushed at his chest; he refused to let her go.

Instead, he thought of their first kiss and of every kiss since. There had been so few. He wanted to spend a lifetime in her arms, showing her exactly how he felt without words.

He remembered her flavor in the darkness, how she smelled in the light. He heard the sounds of her laughter, her anger, her fear. Though her body was soft, her will was strong. She was everything he'd ever searched for, and he was never going to let her go.

Bobby poured everything he felt into the embrace. If she wouldn't believe what he said, maybe she'd believe what he did.

She stopped struggling, started melting. Her arms crept around his neck, her lips opened, and his cell phone rang.

Gasping, she tore away from him. Her fingers went to her mouth, her eyes were glittery with tears. He cursed, yanked the phone off his belt and glanced at the display. This was why he hated cell phones.

He was tempted to ignore the call, but he refrained. The colonel would only keep calling until he answered. Best get it over with.

"Sir?" he said.

"I need you in Uzbekistan immediately. Huge trouble."

"There always is. Get someone else."

"I want you."

"I'm not leaving Mexico until Jane marries me."

Silence met his statement. "I've about had enough, Luchetti. Choose. Her or your job."

"I choose her, sir."

He ended the call, turned off the cell phone, though he doubted the colonel would be calling him back, then glanced at Jane, who was staring at him with an odd expression.

"What?" he asked.

"You really do love me."

"That's what I've been saying."

"Talk is cheap. You gave up Delta for me."

He had. He hadn't even thought about the consequences; all he'd thought about was her.

Jane hurried across the hut, and Bobby opened his

arms. But instead of kissing him, she grabbed his cell phone and punched the on button.

"Call him back."

"Huh?"

"Tell him you were confused. Bad connection. Brain fart. Whatever. You aren't going to stop being soldier boy for me."

He stared into her eyes and he knew the truth. "You really do love me, don't you?"

"Yes," Jane said. "I do."

EPILOGUE

JANE SAT ON THE BEACH and watched the day begin.
By tonight she would be Mrs. Robert Luchetti—or
was that Mrs. Captain Dr. Luchetti?—she couldn't
decide.

A yip from the surf drew her attention. There
were mutations all over the place. Lucky had given
birth to five puppies. Long legs, big heads, at least
they all had eyes—some were spotted, some were
gray, some curly-haired and some straight. Each and
every one was so ugly they were cute.

"You ready?"

She turned to find Bobby's dad standing behind
her. She hadn't had much chance to talk to John.
Guess now was going to be the time.

He sat next to her in the sand. "I got up with the
cows for so many years, can't seem to break that
habit."

"I like the dawn," she said.

"Me, too."

They sat in silence, watching the puppies chase
the waves.

"You gonna keep 'em all?" he asked.

"Yes."

In Mexico, owning seven dogs was not an oddity.

John was working his way up to something, but Jane wasn't sure what. She let him get there on his own.

"I appreciate your attitude about Bobby's job."

"Attitude?"

"I know his mom wanted you to keep him in Mexico, or preferably in a glass box in Illinois."

"She wasn't serious."

"I wouldn't be so sure of that."

Jane smiled. "She's his mom."

"Yeah. But he belongs on the job. He's good at it. We need him there."

"True. Just like they need me here."

John put his hand over hers. "You're perfect together."

She turned and met his eyes. "Thanks."

She and Bobby had decided she'd stay in Mexico for now, and he'd keep doing what he did best. Though they'd be separated a lot, it was better than not being together at all.

"One more thing—"

Jane tilted her head.

"Knock-knock."

"Who's there?"

"Dad."

"Dad who?"

"Dad fuel to the fire."

He was waiting for her to laugh, but she had to admit, "I don't get it."

His shoulders slumped. "You're one of theirs."

"Mine," Bobby said, his shadow falling over her feet. "She's mine."

Jane glanced up and braced for the punch in the gut she felt every time she looked into his blue eyes. She wasn't disappointed.

"You wanna call me Dad—" John stood "—that would be great."

She smiled as he returned to the hotel built high on the bluff. "Your father's a nice man."

"The nicest." Bobby dropped down in the sand. "When he says I can call him Dad, does that mean 'welcome to the family'?"

"No. When he tells you a knock-knock joke, then you're in." Bobby linked his fingers with hers.

"But I didn't get it. I didn't laugh."

"Neither do I."

Bobby watched the dogs frolic in the surf. "Sorry about your mom."

Raeanne had opted out of flying to Mexico for the wedding. She had her hands full saving her career.

"I'm not," Jane said. "The only person I need at my wedding is you."

"Sorry about *my* family then."

The Luchettis had come en masse. The small resort Jane had rented on the Pacific coast was full of them.

The only family members missing were Aaron, Nicole and their daughters. They'd been unable to leave a halfway house full of runaways behind.

Evan and his wife, Jilly, had arrived and announced that they were expecting, too. Luchettis were busting out all over the place.

Kim had agreed to be Jane's matron of honor. The two of them had become great friends, and now they'd be sisters, which was almost as great a gift as Bobby himself.

Colin was going to be Bobby's best man, which was as it should be. The brothers seemed to have gotten over their discomfort with each other and re-turned to the close relationship they'd always shared.

"I like your family," Jane said.

"Even Marlie?"

Jane thought back to her meeting with Colin's wife at the airport. Awkward at first, everything had smoothed out when Tim asked, "Dad says you guys are gonna mud wrestle for Uncle Bobby. So where's the mud?"

Jane and Marlie had started to laugh as Colin and Bobby chased Dean out of the airport and into the Mexican sun.

"*Especially* Marlie," Jane said.

What was there to be jealous about when they'd each gotten the man they were meant to have?

"I love you," Bobby said.

"Right back atcha."

They were married on the beach as the sun went down, with all of the Luchettis surrounding them. As the minister pronounced them husband and wife, everyone clapped.

And Bobby's cell phone began to ring.

"Tomorrow," he said into the receiver. "The world will have to wait until tomorrow."

Bobby tossed the cell phone to Dean, swept Jane into his arms and headed up the bluff, as the world waited and his family cheered.

* * * * *

Look for Dean Luchetti's story,
THE MOMMY QUEST, in 2006!

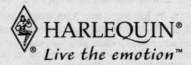

HARLEQUIN *Super*ROMANCE®

is pleased to present a new series by
Darlene Graham

The Baby Diaries
**You never know where
a new life will lead you.**

Born Under The Lone Star
**Harlequin Superromance #1299
On sale September 2005**

Markie McBride has kept her secret for eighteen years.
But now she has to tell Justin Kilgore, her first love,
the truth. Because their son is returning to Five Points,
Texas—and he's in danger.

Lone Star Rising
**Harlequin Superromance #1322
Coming in January 2006**

Robbie McBride Tellchick had three growing boys and
a child on the way when her husband died in a fire. No
one knows how she's going to get along now—except
Zack Trueblood, who has secretly vowed to protect the
woman he's always loved.

*And watch for the exciting conclusion,
available from Harlequin Signature Saga, July 2006.
Available wherever Harlequin books are sold.*

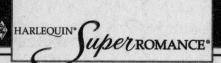

HARLEQUIN *Super* ROMANCE®

Big Girls Don't Cry

by
Brenda Novak

Harlequin Superromance #1296
On sale September 2005

Critically acclaimed novelist
Brenda Novak brings you another
memorable and emotionally engaging
story. Come home to Dundee, Idaho—
or come and visit, if you haven't
been there before!

On sale in September
wherever Harlequin books are sold.

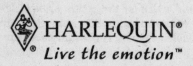

HARLEQUIN®
Live the emotion™